I0567797

This edition first published in the United States in 2011
by North Medina Media

.

124 Doray Drive, Pittsburgh, PA 15237 / www.NorthMedinaMedia.com.
Copyright ©2011 by David Alfred Dalessandro

Library of Congress Cataloging in Publication Data
Dalessandro, David Alfred
Dreamboat by Lila Valentine Thibideaux/by David Alfred Dalessandro
1.   Teenage girls—Fiction 2. Coming of Age—Fiction

Printed in the United States
ISBN 978-0615476155

For Jennie and Al
May they still be dancing

Anadiomene
Via Aurelia
58015-Ortobello, Italy

Ciao Aunt Rowena—

Abusing a corpse?

Those words send a chill up my spine. I
understand your embarrassment concerning my alleged
involvement in this matter.

I agree with you that I have a bit of
explaining to do regarding the events of this past
summer.

I just can't find the words for that yet.

Arrivederci,

Lila

P.S. I hoped you enjoyed the capella du preti.

Anadiomene
Via Aurelia
58015-Ortobello, Italy

Aunt Rowena—

Palm Beach Lolita?

Now I'm upset.

Lolita was only twelve years old and Humbert
Humbert was her stepfather. I was seventeen and A.
was not related to me in the least.

As for the gals down at the Club Coral, I
suppose they don't have anything to do but count
their jewels and jabber like jays anyway. I think its
best you politely tell them to mind their own
business.

Have the police stopped that nonsense about
"abusing a corpse?" I gave Vincenzo, our chef, the
basic facts of the matter and he is honored to work
with Americano dapprima nemico pubblico (that's
"American Public Enemy Number One" but doesn't it
sound romantic in Italian?)

Since you demand to know the details of my
current living arrangements, I am more than willing
to oblige.

"Anadiomene" or, "rising from the sea", is a
resort located on a peninsula named Ortobello. It's
more or less shaped like a boat (the peninsula, that

is), an uncanny coincidence considering my recent history.

The resort consists of a small apartment building, main house and converted barn. My job is to serve meals and clean the rooms. I am basically a maid but that does not bother me in the least. Mrs. Monteverdi speaks excellent English, as do many of the guests.

My Italian is passable. Being a Romance language, it's in the same ballpark as French, so I wasn't totally lost in the beginning. Vincenzo helps by refusing to speak English to me (sort of like learning to swim by being thrown into a lake.)

I live in a room with white plaster walls and a wide-planked floor the color of chocolate. My mattress is as lumpy as bad mashed potatoes. A dresser holds my underwear, slacks and blouses and an armoire my two dresses.

My books are neatly arranged according to height on my writing table, held in position by cast-iron horse bookends. The windows reach from the floor to the ceiling and have gauzy curtains hung from thick metal rods.

Sometimes at sunset, when pink smears the horizon, I fling open the windows. The sound of the breeze against the curtains reminds me of wind luffing against a mainsail and I tear up something terrible.

When this happens, I lift the lid of A.'s travel trunk (it sits at the foot of my bed.) The scent of leather, nicotine and bay rum reminds me I have no reason to wallow in my sorrow. How many eighteen-year-old girls from the wrong side of the tracks summer in Palm Beach and end up halfway across the world in Tuscany, footloose and fancy-free? (Well, I have no idea how many exactly but you catch my drift.)

I hope this letter finds you well. Have you heard word of Harold?

Arrivederci,

Lila

Anadiomene
Via Aurelia
58015-Ortobello, Italy

Ciao, Aunt Rowena!

Your recent letter made me realize that no one will let e'scandoloso di Lila drop until I reveal every last detail of what happened last summer. I am not angry with you in the least and truly believe you deserve to know the real story. I suppose I was naïve in thinking the matter would just go away.

I informed Mrs. Monteverdi of my intention to write a book. A computer was out of the question for reasons far too complex to go into here, but she lent me an ancient Royal portable typewriter with English letters. She said it was A.'s and I have no way of knowing whether that is true. The white letters on the keys were faint, eroded from years of use.

The Royal is quite different from using a computer because of the sounds it makes. The first was a thump deep down inside, followed by the thwack of the letters against the paper.

I thump-thwacked a quarter of the book before the black ribbon dried up. Mrs. Monteverdi showed me how to use the red half of the ribbon next and that got me to the halfway point. She took me to Florence for a holiday and I tried to buy a ribbon, but the typewriter was so old that there wasn't one to fit.

The man at the stationary store asked me if I was a writer and I said I was writing a love story, an adventure and a tragedy all wrapped up in one. He sold me some ink and a box of nice paper and wished me luck.

I used A.'s tortoise shell pens, of course. At first, I suffered a crick in my neck and numb fingers from holding the pen, but after a while I got used to being hunched over for an hour or two at a time.

I finished the book in longhand and even though it doesn't look professional at all, what with half of it typed in black and red and half hand-written, every word of it is true.

And that counts for something.

"DREAMBOAT"

by

Lila Valentine Thibideaux

1

The story I am going to tell is about what I did last summer, just before I turned eighteen. It is about how I went to live with my aunt, Miss Rowena Thibideaux of the Louisiana Thibideaux, in Palm Beach and met a man named Antonio Garibaldi.

I don't know how old he was exactly, but he was five months older than the day I met him when I set his body afire and watched it burn down to ashes.

2

I am the illegitimate daughter of Denton Thibideaux II. He met my mother, Gina Luginbill, when she was a showgirl in Las Vegas. He stayed around long enough to sign my birth certificate and that was the last Mother saw of him.

I don't know how Mother learned that Denton II had died. Since they were never married and never lived together, she had no legal claim on his money. However, she thought I should inherit something just the same.

We talked to a lawyer who found it all interesting, but after investigating matters further, said we might as well spit in the wind than file a lawsuit in St. Charles Parish, where the Thibideaux clan and judges were thick as thieves.

"One day we are going to pay a visit on your Aunt Rowena Lila Thibideaux in Palm Beach so she can see the state her brother left his daughter in."

That was her favorite phrase. One day we were going to do all sorts of things. I finally figured it was the same *one day* she kept talking about and that day just never came.

Because Mother had a steady job in Vegas, we lived in a two-bedroom apartment just off what they call the "old" Strip where smaller casinos were located. The "new" strip had places like the Bellagio that seemed like small cities all by themselves.

I don't know exactly how and why Mother's career as a showgirl ended, but when it did, we became hermit crabs. Hermit crabs have no exterior shell and so must find discarded shells to live in. They are very vulnerable creatures. We were forever moving from one apartment with torn wallpaper and leaky pipes to another because Mother could not seem to find happiness as a career waitress.

In between leases, we lived in a dirt-washed brown station wagon with all our possessions, sometimes staying in motels but mostly sleeping in the car until it broke down for good and that was how we ended up in Lubbock, Texas.

The car died in front of Red's Auto Sales. Red put the station wagon up on a lift and about twenty minutes later came out, wiped his hands on a red towel and announced, "I could save it, but it wouldn't be worth the cost. Might I buy you two lovely ladies lunch?"

Red was a hard-working, decent man. His hair was blonde going on orange, not unattractively so. The thick hair on his forearms covered a million freckles. We'd have been better off if we had stayed with him. Well, Mother would have, for sure.

As luck would have it, Red's wife ran off with his top salesman the Christmas before we met him. Red liked to joke that he came out ahead, since he got rid of his wife *and* didn't have to pay the salesman's Christmas bonus. Red was the "Hi-Value, Low-Cost" dealer in Lubbock, or at least that's what his matchbooks said.

After that first lunch, Mother linked her arm through Red's and they wandered off, shoulders touching. We moved in that very day. We ended up staying for almost a year.

Red owned a rambling wreck of a house surrounded by a few acres of scrubby land. On Sunday afternoons, he would sit on the porch and play music with his friends. The things Red could do with his sax! His music reminded me of a snake with the way it sort of crawled through the air, smooth and muscular. After a while, Red taught me a few Fats Waller tunes. He got a kick out of that, since I was all of eleven singing torch songs like

Ain't Misbehaving and *Keeping Out of Mischief Now.* That was when I realized I could carry a tune, though I didn't do much with the realization except sing in the shower.

The advantage of having Red as a boyfriend was you always had a Hi-Value, Low-Cost car at your disposal (and don't think Mother didn't consider that before deciding to move in with him.) Anyway, something happened in Lubbock that I used to think summed up my childhood.

I refer to it as "The Day the Dog Fell on the Car."

One July day Mother and I got into a mint green 1967 Plymouth Fury Red had just taken in on trade. It had rusty bumpers mostly hidden behind faded stickers, stuff like DON'T LAUGH IT'S PAID OFF. We headed into town for Mother's hair appointment.

When Mother drove, she hunched forward so her nose nearly touched the top of the steering wheel. She seemed cramped and uncomfortable, as she always did when she had to make a decision. And let's face it, driving is nothing if not decision after decision.

Deep drainage ditches edged the narrow dirt road to town and more often than not, we'd find ourselves behind a hay wagon, tractor or some other road-hogging, slow-moving farm vehicle.

On this particular day, the air was scalding hot and thick with dust. The air-conditioning wheezed like it had whooping cough, but it wasn't pushing any cool air.

"The air conditioning isn't working," I said.

"It's running," Mother replied.

"But it's not *working*."

Mother clenched her jaw and I sensed she was trying to will the air conditioner to life. I knew that wouldn't work so I rolled down my window and stuck my head out.

We ended up trapped behind a pickup. I marveled at the sheer amount of junk piled in the back of that truck: a brass headboard, three or four cardboard boxes, a wheelbarrow, a barrel filled with rakes and shovels and other garden implements, a guitar, a rocking chair, a rusted car fender, a sled and an old console television.

The junk was secured with rope trussed this way and that over the contents and tied to the bumper.

"Pass this guy up, Mother," I snapped.

"No passing zone. He'll pull off soon."

Without warning, the truck slammed on its brakes. Mother followed suit. The truck's load shifted, forward and then backward. From somewhere within the junk, a brown dog flew through the air and landed upright on the hood of our car.

Now that's not the sort of thing you see every day.

Just beyond the truck, I noticed a jackrabbit cross the road and disappear into the high grass. The truck drove off.

The dog stared at us through the windshield with red-rimmed eyes, lips drawn back over yellow, mottled teeth, uncertain what it should do next. As the poor creature struggled to remain upright, I heard the distinct sound of claws scratching against the car's finish.

"Beep the horn," I offered.

Mother nodded quickly and beeped the horn twice, which set the dog off on a vicious round of barking. Flecks of foamy spittle speckled the windshield.

The dog flopped down on the hood, lifted its leg and began to lick itself, the sight of which made me sick to my stomach.

"Look away, honey. I'm going to start moving."

The instant the car crept forward, the dog leapt back into action, scrambled onto all fours and barked furiously.

A station wagon passed slowly to the right. The driver stared at the dog and then accelerated, obviously concluding that folks with a dog on their hood needed more help than he was prepared to offer.

An eternity seemed to pass. The engine ticked as it cooled

down. The dog was again licking itself. The heat inside the car was unbearable. My skin grew sticky with sweat.

I couldn't work up the nerve to get out of the car. The dog wasn't large, but it was mangy and ill-tempered, like the boys in school that tormented me.

"Here's the truck," Mother said, relieved. "He's coming back."

A pickup approached from the other direction and passed us.

"Do you believe that?" I said. "He didn't stop."

"Maybe it isn't the same truck."

"It is the same truck, Mother!"

The truck backed up. A hefty man wearing bib overalls and a greasy Dallas Cowboy's ball cap descended from the cab and huffed over to my side. His face was beet-red and scarred, as though someone had shot him with a load full of buckshot. "Got a problem?"

"Your dog is on our hood!" I shouted.

The man grinned and glanced at the dog. He lowered his face so that it was level with mine. "No, it ain't." His breath smelled like a wet cigarette.

"What do you mean, it ain't? It fell out of your truck!"

The man's eyebrows danced furiously. "It ain't my dog."

"Are you sure?" Mother asked.

"'Course I'm sure. I ain't got no dog!"

Horns sounded impatiently behind us.

"Excuse me sir, can you get the dog off our hood?" Mother implored.

The man took a step back, removed his cap and ran his hand over his mostly bald head. He took a step toward the dog and said "Skedaddle" as he waved his hand. I knew that was not going to work. Sure enough, the dog drew back its gums and growled. I felt sorry for the dog because it was obviously scared and confused but that was no excuse for sitting on the hood of our car.

The man went back to his truck and grabbed a baseball bat from the front seat. He got a running start and swung the bat as though it were a sledgehammer. The dog saw him coming and ran in place but managed to get moving just as the bat crashed onto the hood, leaving a horrible dent. Mother screamed and I watched the dog scurry into the tall grass, turn for a final glance, and then disappear.

"Happy?" the man said and walked back to his truck.

I shouted after him. "Hey mister, you got to fix our car now!" but the dusty truck rumbled away. "Mother, are you just going to let him drive away?"

You know the answer to that question. There is no point in analyzing this story further, because it speaks for itself, except to say that although I did not realize it at the time, life was telling me I should not be surprised by anything that happened to me.

And I wasn't.

3

There are five photographs I carry in the inside pocket of my green book bag.

One. Denton II stands next to a shiny red Jaguar sports car. He is wearing white pants and short-sleeved brown shirt, open at the collar. His skin is pale, almost transparent. He is thin and tall.

Two. Mother is all of thirty-two, and I am a few days old. From her blonde hair to the vaguely Oriental slant of her eyes, Mother looks exactly like Faye Dunaway. I look like Winston Churchill. Without the cigar.

Three. I am seven and dressed like a cowgirl. My two front teeth are missing. Mother still looks like Faye Dunaway, although she is a brunette in this picture. She crouches next to me, her hand flat against her brow, shading her eyes. A man's shadow slants across us. I guess you could say men moved through Mother's life like phantoms, leaving only the slightest evidence of their existence.

Four. My seventh grade school photo. We had no money to pay for the basic package of one eight-by-ten, four five-by-sevens and twelve wallet size, so I cut mine out from the yearbook in the school library when no one was looking. I am gawky and goofy-looking (not that the lighting was all that professional, mind you). I am wearing a checkered blouse. My hair looks like I just rolled out of bed. The photo is black-and-white and tiny. That photo fairly shouts out, "Lila Thibideaux is insignificant, her life dull beyond belief!"

Five. I am dressed in a navy blue strapless semi-formal dress Mother picked up at a second-hand store. I have a corsage on my wrist. My date is Benny Carmichael. He stands stiff as a soldier at attention. He was nice enough, I suppose. He was too shy to kiss me goodnight so I gave him a sloppy kiss on my own.

You know, just for the experience.

4

I stand about five-foot-eight. After this beanstalk phase, when I was ten or eleven, my body filled out nicely.

One of Mother's boyfriends once told me I had "legs that wouldn't quit." I take that to mean they are long compared to my upper torso, because otherwise they end at my waist like all human beings. Like Mother, my hair is naturally blonde and I wear it shoulder length now, although at various times I cut it short and dyed it red, purple, and white, though not at the same time. My eyes are blue and I have always been very happy with the shape of my nose.

For a long time, I hated the sound of my own voice. (Red Dakota used to call me "Smokey." He said my voice sounded like I'd smoked cigarettes for fifty years.)

First day of school each year, my new teacher would ask me if I felt okay, because of my voice being so husky. My voice also has a catch in it and swallows a letter or two every sentence. I was self-conscious about talking at all. Most folks just figured I was either shy or mentally stunted when I was younger.

I was neither. In point of fact, I never got lower than an 'A' at any level of mathematics and consider it one of my true natural abilities.

When I was in third grade, we changed school districts in mid-year. I had double pneumonia and then a case of strep. I missed so much time the school recommended I be held back. We moved to another town over the summer, though. Mother told my new principal we were newly arrived from Alaska and so I started fourth grade while they waited for the school records that never came.

Now Mother couldn't find Alaska on a map if you

spotted her the Bering Strait, so we both knew her story was a bald-faced lie. I called her on it and she just told me to never mind because in a thousand years no one would care whether I was held back.

In a thousand years, no one would even know we ever *existed*, let alone whether I was held back in third grade, but it didn't make any sense to argue.

5

Mother had a picture of herself before a show. She looked like a twinkling stork, covered as she was with sequins and feathers and with those legs that would not quit. She had been "Miss Sweet Potato Queen" at sixteen and a year later "Miss Morning Glory." (Ironically, the Morning Glory is a tuber from the same family as the Sweet Potato, so she won the same award twice, the way I figure it.)

She still had the ribbons and trophies. This happened in Georgia where she was born and raised. Right after she graduated from high school, her parents died in an auto accident and she headed for Hollywood but only made it as far as Vegas.

Other than dancing, Mother had no skills to speak of and as we all know, being a former Miss Sweet Potato Queen and four bucks will get you an iced caramel macchiato. (Red Dakota was fond of saying that if he had known folks would wait in line twice as long for the honor of paying twice as much for half as much coffee as they used to, he'd be a millionaire.)

After we left Red for reasons I never understood we lived in small towns in Arkansas and Mississippi. Mother could always find a job as a waitress, sometimes at chains like Denny's and sometimes at Mom and Pop restaurants. After work, she'd dump her tips on the table. I'd count it up, stacking the bills and coins in neat piles. Every so often, she came home late with two fifties or five twenties and no change. She explained she'd met a big tipper and then took a very long shower. I know now what she was up to but I'm not one to pass judgment, considering recent events.

Mother was born and raised in what they call the Bible Belt but had no patience for religion, or as she liked to say, "the blood of the Lamb and such." As a result, I have never set foot inside a church.

Mother worshiped the movies instead. I think we might have had cable for maybe three months of our life. It was a luxury we just could not afford.

Mother believed she could have made it in Hollywood if only she hadn't stopped in Vegas and ended up with someone she referred to only as HIM; as in, "If I had walked the other way when I saw HIM coming, my life would have been different."

Best I could figure he was a gangster of some sort. Mother lived with Him for a while before he threw her out and, instead of just continuing on to Hollywood, she became a showgirl and eventually met Denton.

We had a television. A thirteen-inch with a handle and antenna built into the top. My job was to swing the antenna about until Mother was satisfied with the reception. "A little to the left, no too far, now you moved it too far the other way, back just a teeny bit. . ."

She'd pick a movie over a game show any day, especially an old one like *Double Indemnity* with lots of double-crosses and generally untrustworthy people.

Whenever we could, we'd catch a matinee at the Bijou or Regent or whatever they named the local theater if it wasn't boarded up with FOR SALE or FLEA MARKET SATURDAY on the marquee. Worn, scratchy seat cushions. Sticky cement floor beneath your shoes. Sometimes a balcony. Dark red velvet curtains. A tear or two in the screen. Dust swirling in the shaft of light from the projection booth.

We took our seat as close to the middle as possible. On a weekday matinee in a town of two thousand, you more or less had the place to yourself.

I'd glance over at her face, uplifted and bathed in the

flickering quicksilver light. We always shared a small popcorn, and sometimes she would be so engrossed in the story she would have a kernel poised outside her open mouth for the longest time, spellbound.

I do believe she went to the movies to remind herself what could have been. Not that she intended to do anything about it, because what could have been always was good enough for her.

6

We moved to Philadelphia when I was fifteen because Mother met someone who knew someone who needed a "spokesperson" for the Vita-Juicer.

She took photos in one of the arcade booths and sent them to a man named Earl T. Scomes. She had a few long conversations on the phone with him and before I knew it, we headed north.

Earl sold Vita-Juicers at home shows throughout the Northeast. The Vita-Juicer was equipped with a "heavy-duty industrial motor and surgical-steel cutting blades" that ground up whatever you wanted into juice that was supposed to keep you forever young.

He assured us the television commercials were "in the works." He was shaped like a pear, parted his rust-colored toupee down the middle and grunted whenever he moved, not exactly a ringing endorsement for the Vita-Juicer.

Our first sales trip was to Reading, Pennsylvania, in a white van filled to the brim with Vita-Juicer boxes. He arranged them into a chair for me. Both he and Mother smoked, but only he talked on the way to Reading.

In between telling Mother his life story, (a great portion of which had something to do with the C.I.A. and Kazakhstan), he practiced his sales talk. As far as I was concerned, when it came to salesmanship, Earl was lost as a ball in high grass.

Not only did he not sell a single Vita-Juicer that day, he also exposed himself to me behind a curtain while my mother was packing up the display. He just whipped out his willy and stood there grinning, for gosh sakes!

I didn't bat a lash but looked him right in the eye and said, "I've seen bigger on *dogs*, Mr. Scomes and you are lucky there isn't a surgical-steel cutting blade within my reach."

I told mother and she wanted to leave and not cause trouble. She acted embarrassed, as though we were the ones who had committed a crime and that just set me off.

I told Mr. Scomes, "If you do not pay us for three days work and the cost of a bus ticket back to Philadelphia, I will turn you into the local police. You know what happens to pear-shaped-child-molesters in prison, Earl?" The color drained from his face, and he paid up on the spot.

However, when we went to get our suitcases it was already dark and raining. Earl flung our bags out of the van and sped away. One of the bags popped open, and we had to scurry around in the parking lot gathering up our bras and whatnots.

When we found a pair of Mother's white thong panties lying in a pool of oily water, she slumped down on the curb. I sat next to her and gave her a hug.

I didn't say anything but I thought that a pair of white thong panties sitting an oil slick in some dark, wet abandoned parking lot in Reading, Pennsylvania pretty much summed up our life at that moment.

7

We returned to Philly. Mother went back to her career as a waitress, but only long enough to fall hard for a truck driver, carpenter or welder who was handsome in a rugged sort of way; tall with a full head of hair and in pretty good shape physically. She had a real fixation on broad-shouldered men who made their living with their hands, because she never once came home with a fat, bald accountant.

From what I can tell, broad-shouldered men who work with their hands also suffer from congenital erections. I suppose being pawed all night helped Mother ignore the fact that she was closing in on fifty. Her butt wasn't tight as a drum anymore, and she had crow's feet growing about her eyes. She spent a lot of time staring at her old pictures, as though that would make her young again.

They'd be all lovey-dovey for a few weeks. Then there were long phone conversations with Mother whispering so I couldn't hear what she was saying. I knew when Mother sat red-eyed at the table and watched the cigarette smoke rise toward the ceiling her new love affair had ended.

The world returned to its natural state, meaning just her and me. I was fine with that but Mother without a man was like a stove without a burner.

So she went right out and found herself another man.

8

Luther Henderson combed his thick jet-black hair straight back. He liked Camel cigarettes, Waylon Jennings music, black jeans and white muscle shirts. He had a single word tattooed on his upper arm: *ME.* He was six-foot-three and attractive in that sort of outlaw-biker-bully way; a born bad boy with some indefinable anger smoldering deep within that could burst into flame without warning.

Luther had names for things that already had names. His

cowboy boots were "shit-kickers," his silver-and-turquoise ring a "face-buster" and his SUV a "pussy wagon." Luther even had a name for himself.

The Idea Man.

As far as I can tell that meant he woke up with a big idea in the morning, talked about it all day and completely forgot about it by the time he woke up the next morning with a new big idea.

They say two people can get different things out of the same relationship. Luther was at least fifteen years younger than Mother and I guess that made her feel young and sexy again.

For Luther, Mother was the best audience he ever had. She just hung on his every word. After a while, I figured my mother didn't have a single idea of her own left in her brain, because Luther's had pushed them all out. When I mentioned Luther was in love with the sound of his own voice, she said, "Never you mind. I'm not about to let this one get away."

He had a regular job down at the docks, driving a loader, so at least he was responsible enough to go to work every day.

After three weeks, Mother sat me down and cleared her throat.

"We are going to move in with Luther."

"I'm not moving in with Luther."

"Now honey, he's got a bigger place with cable and all. It's best for us."

I had no idea how having one hundred and fifty-five channels of cable made my life one bit better.

"Are you going to marry that clown?" I asked.

"I'd appreciate it if you called him by his name," she replied.

"Are you going to marry that clown Luther?"

Mother was not amused.

Right after that, in Biology class, I saw a video of an amoeba surround a paramecium and digest it. I shuddered as the paramecium, a helpless organism, simply ceased to exist and became part of the amoeba.

That night, I made one last attempt to convince Mother we should not move in by using the amoeba-paramecium analogy.

"What do amoebas have to do with anything?"

"If we move in, Mother, we will be absorbed like paramecium. We will never be able to separate from Luther."

She kept packing as though she hadn't heard a word I said.

We moved in. Mother seemed happier than she'd been in a long time.

I didn't trust Luther as far as I could throw him. He was always barging into the bathroom when I was taking a shower or into my room when I was getting dressed. He'd make a big deal about apologizing but I knew he did it on purpose. He was out of the house early though and didn't come home until after six during the week so life was bearable. And, of course, we had 155 channels of cable.

Luther had a friend named Dusty. I had no idea what he did for a living but he and Luther went out every Friday night. Dusty wore a fringed leather jacket, ten-gallon cowboy hat, tight jeans and cowboy boots. He stood inside the doorway with his hands shoved into his pockets while Luther ran around looking for his cigarettes, lighter and wallet, one of which he was always missing.

One day Luther came home shit-faced and announced he had been laid-off. He didn't go out and find another job though. Instead, he sat with a can of beer and pack of Camels and remoted through the channels until he found an infomercial. It didn't matter what they were selling, he'd always mutter, "I thought of that first. I should be a millionaire instead of being fucked over by the union bosses. Fuck, I thought up the iPod."

If I was in the room he'd glance over at me and ask, "You don't believe me, do you?" to which I would just roll my eyes and leave and he'd yell after me, "Well, I did, goddamn it!"

About a month later, out of the blue, boxes of new computer equipment were delivered to the apartment. Luther was like a kid in a candy shop. "We are in business! We are going to make money hand-over-fucking-fist!"

"I thought you were unemployed. How you gonna pay for that?" I asked.

"Dusty staked me," he replied.

What *we* were in business doing was running a web site named JAILBAIT.COM, the purpose of which should not require further explanation.

Luther liked to say that I had one perfect little ass and so it will come as no surprise to you that my perfect little ass was what folks were seeing the first few weeks he was in business, being as my perfect little ass was the sole asset of his new company. Not to worry, Luther explained. Dusty was responsible for "securing additional digital content."

I hate thinking about how Mother dragged me into Luther's scheme. Let's just say she made me feel obliged to do my part. Mostly, I wore wigs, short shorts, Catholic schoolgirl skirts, halter-tops, spiked heels, and posed for Dusty. Mother drew the line at me actually posing naked, so I guess she looked out for me in her own way.

9

I was not a very nice person back in Philadelphia. What's done is done. However, I think it's important to know I came to Philadelphia pure as the driven snow and left as cold, dirty slush.

I mostly behaved in school. My junior year I went out for the basketball team because I was tall and thought it might be fun. The coach said I had potential but my skills were raw, and I needed to go to a summer basketball camp if I wanted to play varsity. Mother refused to pay. I drifted away from athletics at that point. I took Driver's Ed and earned my license, though I never drove a car after that.

My senior year I joined the French club and washed cars and such to earn money for a trip to Paris (with the club that is.) I even got a passport. Luther paid the application fee. I never did make that trip to France for reasons that will become apparent.

Back on the private enterprise front, the web was going very well. The entire living room was filled with computers and cables. An Indian guy in a turban named Saj came by now and then. He was very polite but smelled like incense. He was some sort of programming whiz.

Luther bought a new pussy-wagon, a black Lincoln Navigator SUV, and about ten pairs of handmade shit-kickers.

Mother had boxes of stuff coming from Victoria's Secret and The Shopping Network and QVC and such and the boxes started piling up. Then Dusty would come by and take a big load of the stuff out.

I think Luther might have hijacked an entire truckload of iPods because I had a Shuffle, Nano, Classic, Touch, and every upgrade in between. He passed them out like packs of gum.

Luther had a definite man-crush on Steve Jobs. Not a day went by that Luther didn't ask, "What would Steven do in a case like this?" As far as I was concerned, Luther Henderson could sit on a rock and think for a hundred years without ever answering that question.

Luther also bought me an amazing diamond pendant. My share of the profits, he explained. Two seconds later, he tried to seduce me. (I use the word "seduce" loosely, for it is downright embarrassing to see a grown man beg for a blowjob.) I had no interest in that *at all*. I never told Mother about it, though if I had it would have saved me a lot of trouble.

Anyway, someone once said that when one door closes another opens, in a cosmic sense, that is. Fact was, if it hadn't been for JAILBAIT.COM, Mother would not have abandoned me and the rest of this story would never have happened.

10

I was the only one there when the Feds raided the apartment. I was terrified, what with them smashing down the door and shouting "F.B.I!"

It was six in the morning. I stumbled out of my bedroom in a panties and bra. Four agents in blue F.B.I windbreakers stopped short and stared at me as I arranged my arms to cover up best I could. The head agent held up papers and told me he had duly authorized search warrants for the premises and then told me to put some clothes on.

After they carried out all the computers, they asked me if I knew the whereabouts of "certain individuals named Mr. Luther Henderson and Ms. Gina Luginbill."

I told the truth. They were there when I went to sleep the night before.

They asked me how old I was and I said I'd be eighteen on September eighteenth. They asked for my driver's license. Two Agents huddled together, whispered, and finally told me to pack a change of clothes because I was going with them.

I had like ten minutes to decide what I should take with me. I put on the diamond pendant but hid it beneath my shirt. I stuffed as many pairs of clean underwear, tops and socks into my backpack as I could. At the last moment, I remembered the passport and took that too. I felt better having it, in case I had to make a run for the border.

I said I had to go to the bathroom and went inside and started to text Mother on my iPhone. Then I realized the FBI might confiscate the phone and trace Mother's location, so I just took the top off the toilet tank and dropped the phone inside.

They took me to the police station. As I walked in, Dusty came walking out, handcuffed, a man in a suit on either side of him. If he saw me, he didn't let on.

The police put me in a small room with a table and chairs. I was moved three or four times during the day into other rooms. The police station was dirty and noisy and every five minutes someone shouted, "Shut up and sit down!" in the hallway outside.

Around one o'clock a policewoman showed up and apologized left and right for letting me slip between the cracks.

"Let's get you some lunch," she said and took me across the street to a diner.

I ordered a toasted cheese sandwich and a glass of iced tea. After I wolfed it down, I asked the policewoman, "My mother is terrible trouble, isn't she?"

Suddenly, I was aware of someone standing next to me. My guardian angel, Marla Thomas, had just fluttered into my life.

11

Marla drove me to her office at the Bureau of Public Welfare.

"We've got ourselves a little problem. Because you are a minor we need to find you a place to stay."

Her skin was the color of coffee with a whole bunch of cream in it and she was just plump full of love. I liked her right off because she said we had a problem, when, in fact, I was the one that didn't have anywhere to go.

(Now Luther was fond of calling black people "porch monkeys" and "jungle bunnies" and forever going on about how they were the problem with the world and had cost him his job. "What with Affirmative Action and all," he said, as if he had studied law or read anything other than skin magazines on the john. I, for one, will testify Marla wasn't the cause of any problems in the world and certainly wasn't holding Luther back.)

"Can't I go back to the apartment? My mother's probably there waiting for me. She'll be terribly worried."

Marla's face tightened up. "Honey, your mother is a fugitive from a federal felony warrant."

You know those movies where it's the future and everyone is filthy and lives underground in a steamy boiler room? When I realized Mother had abandoned me, it was as though I was walking through a park and the earth opened up and I fell right into that future.

I wasn't about to cry in front of a woman I'd known for an entire hour, even one plump full of love, but that doesn't mean I wasn't downright devastated. I thought Mother and I were best friends, that in the end we could depend on one another. I wanted to believe Luther had poisoned Mother's mind and it was only a matter of time before she came to her senses but she'd run off nonetheless and had to be accountable for that in the end.

I must have teared up but I was so upset I didn't notice. Marla handed me a tissue.

"Do you know what they were doing?"

"Digital erotica?"

Marla shook her head. "The purpose of the website was to fraudulently obtain credit card numbers and use them for unauthorized expenditures. These transactions were conducted across state lines and were federal offenses. Since your mother used these card numbers, she is an accessory, at the very least. "

"Are you sure about this?" I asked. Considering the FBI was already involved that was, in retrospect, a stupid question.

"They allegedly stole over a half-million dollars."

And to think Mother wouldn't pay for summer basketball camp!

Even though my diamond pendant was hidden, it felt hot against my skin because I knew I was in possession of illegally obtained jewelry. I didn't mention it and Marla never asked if I had personally benefited from my mother's crime spree. I know, I know. Shame on me.

Anyhow, I'd seen enough movies to understand the law. You don't mess with the Feds. Even Mafia Dons took it on the chin. Mother was ill-equipped to live out a Bonnie-and-Clyde scenario.

"We have two options here."

"What's the first option?" I cringed as though the answer was a snowball heading my way.

"We can put you in a group shelter. They are clean and safe." Right off, I imagined teenage girls like me chained together in that boiler room, hair wet and stringy, dresses tattered, steam hissing while a fat man with a hairy chest and a studded dog collar cracked a whip.

"What's the second option?"

"We find a family member to take you in. Do you know how to get in touch with your father?"

"He's dead. Anyway, he and Mother never married."

"On your mother's side?"

"Dead too."

"Another relative perhaps? An aunt or uncle?"

"I know what a fucking relative is," I snapped. She cocked her head and looked at me with one eye.

"Child, if I was your mother, I'd put you over my knee and give you a good tanning."

"I know men who would pay good money to watch that."

Marla sat back in her chair. It creaked like it needed a good oiling.

"My, my, child, what have they done to you?"

She shook her head and made this little clicking sound with her tongue against her teeth. Truth was, I was just acting out and had no call to jump all over the one person who wanted to help me.

"I'm sorry. I'm just a little on edge right now."

"I expect you are. Do you have an answer for me? An aunt or uncle?"

Before I knew it, Rowena Lila Thibideaux's name popped into my brain and right out of my mouth.

Aunt Rowena probably didn't know I existed. Even so, I figured it was worth a try. I'd never been in Palm Beach but it had to be better than that boiler room.

Marla's face lit up as if I had just given her a Christmas present. She opened my file and took out an ink pen.

"What's her last name?"

"Thibideaux. Of the Louisiana Thibideaux?"

Marla seemed unimpressed but wrote it down anyway. "Would you happen to know her phone number or address?"

"She lives in Palm Beach. That's all I know."

"And what relationship is she to you exactly?"

"She's my aunt."

"How is that?"

"What do you mean?"

"Is she your mother's sister or your father's sister? Is she really your aunt or is that just a term of endearment?"

"What would that be? A term of endearment?"

"Well, sometimes we call folks 'Aunt' even though they're not blood. When I was growing up, we had a woman who lived down the street. Aunt Clara? It wasn't until she died that I learned she was no kin to me at all."

"She's my father's sister."

Marla closed the file. "You listen to Marla, child. There are two kinds of people in this world. 'Just folks' and 'no-accounts.'"

"No-accounts?"

"A body that doesn't fit into proper society because there is no-accountin' for their behavior. Now some say the good Lord gave me a gift, and that is the ability to spot a no-account right off."

"I believe that."

"And I can tell right off that you are 'just folks'."

There was no-accountin' for a lot of my behavior but if the Lord gave Marla a gift who was I to argue?

12

The shelter was okay. Funny thing was, Marla found out I had already completed my graduation requirements and could have graduated in the previous December. Like I knew I could do that!

I don't remember much else except sitting around and watching one-hundred and fifty-five channels. I thought about Mother a lot at first, but it hurt so badly I forced her from my mind.

I kept my diamond pendant in my panties. I know that sounds gross, but I wrapped it in a hankie. It was uncomfortable but I was afraid of anyone knowing I had it because I figured possession would make me an accessory.

Marla kept in touch. She told me she'd finally been in

touch with Aunt Rowena but nothing had been resolved. I thought about running away and finding Mother on my own but didn't have the energy. I got paranoid and started to believe there was a special air they pumped through the ducts that made you gave up on life and not think to run away. Every girl in the shelter had empty eyes, just staring off into space, unable to focus on anything. Zombies, that's what the air turned us into.

The living dead.

Just when I had about given up completely Marla came to fetch me.

"I have great news, Lila. Your Aunt Rowena has agreed to take you in until your eighteenth birthday."

"She did?" I was totally amazed because for all I knew she'd never heard my name. Marla could work some magic, she could.

At the airport, Marla bought me a Coke and hot pretzel and sat with me at the gate. She gave me her e-mail address and said if I happened to have access to a computer, she'd love to know how I was getting along.

"Excited?" she asked.

"Nervous, mostly. I've never been on a plane before."

"I meant are you excited about meeting your Aunt?"

"Very."

Marla patted my hand. "Everything is going to work out fine. Trust me. Oh, almost forgot." She fished around in her purse and handed me a pair of sunglasses. "I've got a feeling your future's so bright you gonna need these."

It didn't matter if that wasn't an original idea of hers. It made things a little better to know someone had confidence in my future, because I certainly didn't.

When it was time to get on the plane she gave me a big hug.

"Someone will meet you at the airport. He'll be holding a sign with your name on it. Now, you aren't gonna disappoint, are you? You're not gonna go off like some no-account when the plane lands?"

"No ma'am," I said and I suppose I meant it. What I really wanted was for that plane never to touch down because as long as it was in the air I couldn't possibly be disappointed by what I found waiting for me in Palm Beach.

13

The plane landed.

I found a man holding a white cardboard sign with my name neatly printed in magic marker.

"I'm Lila."

"Pleased to meet you, Miss Thibideaux. I am Harold. Do

you have any luggage?"

Harold Edgerton Grant III was about fifty years old and actually shorter than I was. His skin looked freshly scrubbed, very pink, and his eyes twinkled as though he knew something no one else did. He was bald. He wore a black suit and spoke with a very proper English accent. He looked silly carrying my ratty backpack but he was so serious about doing it, I couldn't help but love him right off.

When I stepped outside the terminal a fist of hot air punched at me. The sun was terribly bright and all the sudden I felt the need to barf in the worst way. The whole world slowed down as we walked toward this long, shiny, black car.

I reached for my sunglasses but the world started spinning and a woman screamed and everything went dark.

When I came to, I was lying on the ground. Harold cradled my head.

"You've had a fainting spell, I fear."

I felt completely refreshed, as though I'd slept for twelve hours. A crowd of people had gathered about me but parted to allow a paramedic through. He asked me whether I was on medication and the last time I ate. He checked my eyes with a little flashlight, took my pulse and my blood pressure. He announced my vital signs were normal and I could be on my way.

Harold helped me to my feet and led me to the black car. I could hear people whispering and it was quite a relief to slide into the cool, dark interior. When the door slammed no one could see me because the windows were tinted. I put on my sunglasses anyway. That was as close to crawling into a dark hole as I could manage.

"A most auspicious entry into Palm Beach society, Miss Lila," Harold said cheerfully. His voice came through speakers next to my ear.

"I am so embarrassed. I have never fainted in my life."

"Perhaps it is your cold."

"I don't have a cold. It's my natural voice."

"There are refreshments in the bar. Please help yourself."

I opened a small refrigerator, removed a Coke and stuck the bottle cap into my purse.

I felt rubbery until I saw the ocean and immediately felt as though someone flicked on my right-as-rain switch.

The houses took my breath away. Most of them were hidden behind cast iron fences or bushes, but every now and then, I caught a full glimpse of one and wondered who could possibly need that much interior space.

We finally stopped in front of a greenish iron gate that

towered over the car.

Harold pointed a remote control and the big gate swung open. My jaw dropped as Aunt Rowena's humongous pink house passed to my left. Technically, it's a classic Renaissance Villa with hand-turned columns and hand-carved balusters and window surrounds of natural stone. Stucco finish over wood framing with an orange ceramic tile roof. Porticos galore.

Harold pulled the car around the back into a brick courtyard with a fountain in the middle. He hustled around and opened my door.

"Welcome to 'Sea Spray'," he said.

The grass was so green it looked artificial. Neat beds filled with red and yellow flowers ringed the courtyard, with not a dandelion to be seen. Brown and white brick swirled outward from the fountain. The fountain wasn't running. The only sound was the roar of the ocean, but it was muffled, like when you hold a shell up to your ear. Salt danced on the breeze but otherwise the air was sparkling clean.

The house towered over me and framed the courtyard. To my left was a four-door garage, each door set under a brick arch. Above the arches was a covered walkway.

In the middle of the back lawn was a small white temple at one end of a long, narrow, incredibly blue swimming pool.

The lawn stretched further on until it reached the ocean.

My eye had a hard time taking it all in as I followed Harold through the back door and into the house.

The kitchen had a gleaming white tile floor, stainless steel counter tops and two stoves. Copper pans hung down from hooks on the ceiling and meat cleavers dangled from a slab of wood with huge legs.

A dark-skinned woman wearing a black dress and white apron washed vegetables in the sink. "Chaco, this is Miss Lila. She is joining us for the summer."

"Hello," I said but Chaco only glanced at me and nodded.

The scale of the house was overwhelming and not the least bit inviting. I lost count of how many rooms we actually passed through. One long, narrow space had circular patterns of pink and black granite on the floor and an elaborately painted *tromp d'oeil* (as I later learned) on the arched ceiling.

Harold's shoes echoed softly on the floor and Sea Spray suddenly reminded me of a museum: cold, deathly quiet and lifeless.

We reached the front entrance. The doors were frosted glass and a statue of a naked woman stood on either side. A crystal chandelier glittered as if it was made of diamonds, and lots of big jungle plants were scattered here and there.

The most amazing thing was a double staircase that changed directions at a landing on the way down. The handrail was made of pinkish marble and a carpet the color of blood covered the stairs. The sun streamed in through an enormous window and fair to blinded me.

Aunt Rowena emerged from that light as she descended the stairs.

It was clear she spent a lot of time in a beauty parlor. In fact, she looked like she just stepped out of one. She sparkled like the chandelier when she walked, but in her case, there was no doubt she was made of real diamonds what with her bracelets, rings and a necklace. (I thought my necklace was a big deal, but it was a mere trinket before Aunt Rowena's baubles.)

She was big. Not fat. Just big, like the center on our girls' basketball team, though I couldn't imagine her sweating. She looked me up and down and smiled like she was chewing glass.

"Now then, child, let me make myself perfectly clear. My dearly departed brother was a blight on the family name, but he did father you and a bastard Thibideaux is a Thibideaux nonetheless. Do not confuse my sense of duty with hospitality. If you do anything during your stay to sully the Thibideaux name, you will be sorry you ever found your way to my door."

I was already sorry.

"Come with me child. You must understand the importance of being a Thibideaux."

She led me through enormous wood doors that slid into the walls. We entered a room paneled in dark wood. The light blue carpet was deep and soft. On the walls were life-sized oil portraits in gold frames.

"This is General Buford Thibideaux," she began, pointing to a man wearing a Confederate uniform. His hand rested on a globe. "A true hero of the Confederacy. He ran Yankee blockades under Letters of Marque signed by Jefferson Davis himself until he was caught and hung from the yardarm of his ship."

I suppose if you are going to fight on the losing side, you might as well be a hero, although I am not certain that being hung from your yardarm qualifies as 'heroic.'

Next was a portrait of a man holding a rifle with two hound dogs at his side. "This is Denton Thibideaux, your father's namesake. He was the first Thibideaux to serve on the Board of Regents at the Louisiana State University. He was an oilman. He ran the company until he was nearly ninety, when he sold his holdings to Gulf Oil."

That explained where all the family money came from, short and sweet.

Next in line: a thin woman sat in a garden with a cat on

her lap. She looked like she had just swallowed vinegar.

"This was Winifred Thibideaux. She wrote poetry and died an old maid. The only man she loved was shot-gunned to death. The trial of the century, they called it, but of course Aunt Winnie was exonerated."

I wondered if the den of thieves in St. Charles parish had anything to do with *that*.

"This is Winnie's brother, Raeford Thibideaux, in his time the most powerful politician in Louisiana."

I stared at a portrait of a man with fierce eyes and a handlebar moustache.

"Was he the governor?""

She sniffed as though the question was an insult. "Oh, he was more powerful than the *Governor*. He was known as 'Black Jack' but I assure you all of his dealings were on the up-and up. He was also on the Board of Regents at the Louisiana State University."

I don't know how a man named Raeford gets the nickname of "Black Jack" or why Aunt Rowena thought it necessary to protect his reputation to a stranger, but it was pretty clear in my mind that nothing he did was on the "up and up."

The next portrait depicted a heavy-set man with cheeks like a bulldog sitting in his armchair with a young boy and girl at either shoulder.

"This is my Daddy Buford. That's your father, Denton and I next to him. I was sixteen. Daddy was on the Board of Regents at Louisiana State University, too."

When Aunt Rowena was young, she was long of bone, like me, and I could see a definite family resemblance in our eyes and the shape of our noses.

"My brother was the black sheep of the family. He impregnated a Louisiana State cheerleader and then forced her to have an abortion. The poor girl died."

She walked away and I followed.

"Daddy was quite disappointed, given his position. He created a trust to provide him with a living allowance and banned him from the state."

It was hard to tell whether Buford was angry because his son embarrassed him or because the poor girl died.

"Is your father still alive?"

"Daddy is going on a hundred, but he's still got his faculties. We Thibideaux are quite long-lived."

Except for my father, that is.

"How did my father die?"

We were back in the entry.

She kept talking while she walked. "He came to a bad

end. That's all you need know."

I would have pressed her for more details, but I figured there would be time enough that summer once I knew Aunt Rowena better.

She was proud of her family but the Thibideaux clan had all sorts of secrets buried in its past. In that respect, they were no better or worse than any other family, except few families have oil portraits of their ancestors. Six-foot tall portraits, that is.

We went to a room with a stained glass dome and sat at a round table with a glass top. Water spurted out of the mouth of an angel nearly buried in more jungle plants. The air inside the room was hot and wet and I thought it was the last place you'd want to sit, but Aunt Rowena didn't seem to mind.

"Would you like anything to eat or drink?"

"Coke and a sandwich will be fine."

She rung a hand bell and Chaco appeared.

"Chaco," Aunt Rowena said over her shoulder, "please bring a Coke and a tuna sandwich for our visitor." She cleared her throat and studied one of her diamond rings, as though something was written there.

"Now then, I am leaving for Bar Harbor immediately and will remain there until the winter season."

You could have hit me upside the head with a two-by-four! Here I was all worried about how Aunt Rowena and I would get along and she wasn't even going to be around.

"You are to follow Harold's instructions without fail. If you comport yourself in a manner unbecoming, Harold has been instructed to send you back to Philadelphia. Am I making myself clear?"

"Yes."

She bustled out of the room. Harold materialized.

"What do you do here, Harold?"

"I thought you understood that I am Miss Thibideaux's manservant."

Like every day I met a manservant, you know?

"How big is this house, anyway?"

"Twenty-one rooms, all told."

"And Aunt Rowena lives here all alone?"

Before he could answer, Aunt Rowena returned, waving a handkerchief in front of her face, as breathless as if she'd just run a hundred-yard dash.

"I fear I've forgotten something, Harold."

"We have checked and double-checked, madam. All is in order."

"Yes, yes. Oh, I do so hate the rigmarole of leaving."

I would have never guessed Aunt Rowena would be

flustered about anything, but here she was, fanning herself and acting like a schoolgirl before her first date.

Harold cleared his throat and nodded toward me. Aunt Rowena waved her hand over her shoulder as she walked way. "Remember, child, that you are a Thibideaux."

"Of the Louisiana Thibideaux," I muttered under my breath.

Chaco arrived with my sandwich and left.

I sat alone in the hot air and decided I did so hate the rigmarole of being abandoned.

14

I was put in the garage.

Not *in* the garage exactly, but in the apartment above. I followed Harold up a flight of stairs and we walked along the covered walkway above the garage doors. He opened the door and ushered me inside.

He raised the blinds and light flooded in through the windows. I could see the ocean, swimming pool and on the edge of the property, a grove of trees.

The furniture was very masculine, made of heavy dark wood. There was a four-poster bed, a dresser with a mirror and a television inside an armoire. On the shelves below were some books, a VCR and video tapes.

"Miss Thibideaux asked me to extend her apologies at her hurried departure," Harold said as he flipped a switch and a ceiling fan began creaking.

"You don't have to lie, Harold. She thinks I'm poor white trash and hates the very thought of me."

"If you have any needs, please ring the service bell," he replied, pointing to a button on the wall. "Lunch is at eleven-thirty. Dinner at five. Breakfast is a moveable feast."

"Do you really think she's sorry she left?"

Harold's body stiffened and he said firmly, but not angrily, "I am completely in Miss Thibideaux's confidence."

By which I took to mean I was never going to learn what my Aunt really thought about anything from Harold.

"One more matter. I live in the main house. Chaco and Magda leave at five-thirty. They set the security code to the house when they depart. If you have need of anything after that hour, ring the service bell." He pointed at an intercom on the wall.

I concluded that was a polite way of saying I was to stay out of the main house after five-thirty.

"Now then, here are your facilities," he said, opening a door.

My bathroom in Philly had a shower inside the tub and a

nasty curtain with mold along the lower edge, grungy orange-and-black plastic tile on the wall and cracked linoleum on the floor. Being as there was no closet, my mother bought a plastic shelving unit where she piled all her makeup and such.

My Palm Beach bathroom was something else entirely! The floor and walls were gleaming white tile with swirls of pink. The tub was set into the floor and had gold faucets shaped like dolphins. The sink had matching faucets, in addition to the face of a woman carved into the front of the bowl.

"This is my bathroom, all to myself?" I asked.

"Indeed. We have stocked the cabinet with a supply of toiletries. I hope we have anticipated your needs. If you have any other requirements, you need only ask. Now, if you have no further questions, I will leave you to your own devices."

After he left, I turned on the television and discovered I had basic cable but no premium channels. I checked out the videos. I was unimpressed. First off, a VCR? You'd think someone as rich as Aunt Rowena could afford a DVD player.

The video selections consisted of a six-tape history of the Second World War and a few movies, none of which I'd seen.

A half hour later, there was a knock at the door and a tiny woman entered. She was dressed like Chaco and wore black shoes that looked just god-awful. Fashion-wise, that is.

"I am Magda. I will draw your bath now." She had a real Bela Lugosi accent thing going.

She started to fill the tub and splashed the water with her hand. "Is okay?"

"Yeah, it's great," I replied, but then realized she wanted me to check the temperature of the water. "I can fill a tub," I said, not wanting to sound harsh.

"I'm Lila." I extended my hand. She didn't take it.

"Yes. Your dirty clothes go in chute," she explained and pushed open a wooden flap door in the wall.

She set out a towel and red satin robe and backed out, pulling the door shut behind her.

I dropped my dirty clothes down the chute. I hid the pendant in a glass jar filled with cotton balls.

I fiddled with the tub water until it was just right and stepped in. On a glass shelf next to the tub was a collection of bath oils and such. I sniffed them, one after another, and dumped a few drops of flowery smelling stuff into the water.

I slid down until the water covered my ears and my hair floated up like a big lily pad. I descended into total silence.

I thought: I am living in a mansion that belongs to a woman who doesn't want me here while Mother is on the lam from a federal warrant. I have people waiting on me hand-and-foot while Mother is living hand-to-mouth. I felt guilty. I felt like a stranger in a strange land. I felt so many things I lost track. I never thought there were so many reasons to feel bad.

I decided to figure out a way to get back to Philadelphia and find Mother. I belonged in Palm Beach as much as Harold belonged on a street corner in North Philly. Since no one wanted me here, I might as well be some place familiar.

On the domed ceiling were painted fluffy white clouds against a baby blue background. Four smiling baby angels peeked out from behind those clouds.

Even though the plump full-of-love baby angels were pink, one of those angels looked exactly like Marla. Her face hit me like a proverbial bolt of lightning. I remembered my promise to her that I would not be a no-account. Breaking my promise to her seemed to be the first step on the short road to being a no-account.

Taking a bath in private without worrying about Luther bursting in was a grand experience. I poured more oils into the water and tried the bubble bath too. I stayed in the bath longer than I had any need to and was pruned up when I climbed out.

I dried off, pulled on the robe and wrapped the towel around my head, turban-style. It was one of the few neat things Mother ever taught me.

The medicine cabinet was indeed stocked with everything I might need. I smeared a green mud masque over my face and sat on a fancy stool. I just closed my eyes and listened to the soft whisper of the air conditioning until the masque dried. After I rinsed off my face, I blew my hair dry, then made up my face.

All this took nearly an hour. When I opened the bathroom doors, Magda was still standing there.

"The bus doesn't stop here anymore," I joked, but she didn't get it.

She went into the bathroom and shut the door. I heard her scrubbing the tub. I peeked inside.

"I don't want you to take this the wrong way, but I'd rather just take care of the tub by myself."

She half-heartedly bowed and left.

I tossed the robe on the bed and pulled on a pair of sweats and a faded blue T-shirt.

As I scrubbed the tub, snatches of my life ran through my mind, like how Mother took her cigarette out of her mouth in the morning before she kissed me on the top of my head, the raggedy teddy bear on my bookshelf I'd had ever since I was five, cleaning the clump of hair out of the tub drain, the argument about whether or not she told me to pick up milk on the way home from school, stupid stuff that wouldn't mean anything to anyone else but me. I mean, it wasn't much of a life but it was all mine.

Suddenly it hit me with the force of a roundhouse right. I was seventeen-going-on-eighteen and my life as I had known it was over. The tears started coming and I couldn't stop them. I fell forward onto the bed and buried my head in the pillow. As far as I was concerned, at that moment, it would be fine if I just curled up and died.

15

I didn't leave the apartment for three days. I had a fever, but it wasn't one you could measure with a thermometer.

I was truly sick at heart.

Sometimes I stared out the window. Vans came and went, bringing men to work on the lawn and flowerbeds, the pool and even to deliver groceries.

The pool boys were more or less my age and strutted around all tanned and muscular. They didn't interest me in the least, for I had decided people simply couldn't be relied upon. The only person I trusted anymore was Marla and she was a thousand miles away. My father had long ago abandoned me. Mother had too, even though it was technically the result of interstate flight to avoid prosecution. Aunt Rowena could not care less about me and she wasn't around anyway.

On top of it all, I got my period. I found what I needed in the medicine cabinet okay, but my period usually made me blue anyway and that just added to my general depression.

I watched two of the videos. They were English movies and very boring. The plots of each revolved around rich English women who had nothing better to do than obsess about who they would marry. Manservants were important characters in both. I understood Harold better after watching.

A cable channel played true crime stories. At least a few hours every day I watched stories about women who should have organized PTA bake sales but instead hired hit men to kill their husbands, or husbands who should have been golfing but killed their mistresses and stuffed their bodies into empty thirty-gallon industrial drums. After you've seen about fifty variations on the same theme, it was hard to be shocked or even fascinated.

When I grew bored, I rolled over and stared at up at the gently turning ceiling fan. Hours could pass just watching those paddles turn round and round.

I cried myself to sleep and woke with a pounding headache, my nose filled with snot. My face was splotched and puffy. I looked like hell. I didn't change clothes. I soon was aware of my body's vinegary stench.

Usually there was a silver tray of food on my bed stand when I woke. I didn't eat anything but toast or crackers. The tray would stay there until I fell asleep and when I woke, it would be gone. It was like living with ghosts and I wondered if maybe there was a video camera somewhere in the apartment.

Sometimes, late at night, I saw a strange yellow glow inside the grove of trees. I thought there was maybe another building on the estate but my interest didn't go beyond that.

I had the crazy thought of not leaving that apartment again. One day someone would wonder what happened to that Lila girl and I would be found, shriveled up, like Norman Bates' mother.

Then, on the fourth day of my depression, everything unexpectedly changed.

I was staring out of the window, my chin resting in my palm. You know, very pensive, although I can't tell you what I was thinking about exactly. Given my state of mind, it was undoubtedly something to do with how to kill Luther in a hot tub and make it look like an accident.

Outside, air was gray, like after a hot shower when you forget to put on the exhaust fan. A man dressed in a tuxedo materialized out of the mist. His coat was slung over his shoulder and a cloud of cigarette smoke trailed along behind.

He came from the direction of the ocean, rather than the street. Before I knew it, he'd disappeared back into the mist as though he never existed.

At that very moment, my entire frame of mind changed.

I am not one for labored symbolism but stay with me. At that very moment, my life was like that mist. Because when you are right in the middle of the mist you can't see all that far ahead and most of the time you're lucky you don't walk into a wall or drop into a hole, which, metaphorically speaking, was what had happened to me a lot lately.

I realized the point of life was to quit worrying about walking into a wall long enough to see a man in a tuxedo walk out of the mist before sunrise.

Now you might ask if that was enough to make me stop feeling sorry for myself and leave the apartment.

Given my life experiences up to that point, it most certainly was.

16

I took a long bath, shaved my legs, blew dry my hair and put on a little make-up.

I finished dressing and noticed a light on in the kitchen of the main house. I stepped outside into the heavy morning air and made my way across the courtyard and into the house.

I found Harold puttering about in black pants, starched shirt and silvery vest.

"Out and about early, I see," he said cheerfully. "Now that you have decided to leave your apartment, there's a small matter to attend to."

He opened a narrow door inside the pantry and flipped on the light. Inside were tiny television monitors showing images on the estate (but none of my apartment) and rows of blinking lights. There were also several spare keys hanging under neatly typed labels. I noticed one key hung under the word 'cottage.'

"This is your apartment key. And while I'm at it, let me give you the code for the keypad on the front gate."

He wrote the combination on a piece of paper and handed it to me.

I stuffed the paper into the pocket of my jeans. "What are you doing up so early yourself?" I asked. "I thought you would sleep in now that my Aunt is gone."

"I rise at five every morning, as I have for all of my adult life. Would you care for breakfast?"

"Oh, God, yes." I was famished.

"Might I suggest a perfect soft-boiled egg, along with toast and marmalade?" He held up two brown eggs. "The important thing is to use eggs at room temperature. Never cook an egg directly from the cooler."

"I'll be sure to remember that."

He rubbed his hands together and then carefully placed the eggs in a pot of boiling water, shut off the gas and covered the pot. He quickly set a timer.

"Five minutes exactly. Not a second too short or too long."

When the timer went off Harold scooped the eggs out of the water and set them in matching blue cups.

"Staffordshire china cups. Quite valuable, as these things go," he explained. He picked them up and carried them to the table as the toast popped out of the toaster. He also gave me a cup of sweet and lemony tea.

"How am I supposed to eat it?" I asked.

Harold picked up a paring knife and sliced away the tip of the egg.

"You only eat half?"

"Oh, you can eat it all, if you so desire. Now then, take your toast soldier and dip."

I picked up a triangular piece of toast and dipped the end into the yolk. "I saw a man cutting across our property. He was wearing a tuxedo."

Harold laughed softly to himself, then set his spoon down and folded his hands in front of him.

"That would be Mr. Garibaldi. He lives in the caretaker's cottage."

"There's a cottage?"

"In the orange grove."

I remembered the odd glow I'd seen in the grove of trees.

"So he's the caretaker?"

"We don't have a caretaker."

"Then why does he live in the caretaker's cottage?"

Harold cleared his throat and poured me more tea. "Mr. Garibaldi is a new addition to the estate. He's been here for three months."

"Where'd he live before?"

"I never saw him before in my life until he moved into the cottage."

"He just appeared and moved into the cottage?"

"Miss Rowena indicated he would be moving in."

"Does he pay rent?"

"He's living off the cuff, so to speak."

"So he doesn't?"

"No."

"How old is he?"

"I met him only once. In my estimation, Mr. Garibaldi is a well-preserved gentleman in his late sixties or early seventies."

"He stayed out all night. Don't you think that's odd for someone that old?"

"My duties do not include taking note of Mr. Garibaldi's comings and goings." He cleaned his fingers on a cloth napkin. "Discretion is my stock in trade, Miss Lila."

I found all of this quite heady stuff, you see, and pressed on breathlessly.

"And you're not the least bit curious about what he does all night? Maybe he's a vampire. They can't stand the sun, you know."

"He's most certainly not a vampire because such notions are poppycock, regardless of the current popular fascination with all matters sanguinary," he replied testily.

He scraped the crumbs off the table with a short ruler and then tugged at the bottom of his vest with both hands. "If you are quite finished with the inquisition concerning Mr. Garibaldi, would you meet me in the courtyard around ten?"

"Why?"

"Miss Thibideaux left instructions for me to take you shopping for appropriate clothing. I think its best we do that now that you no longer have a bee stuck in your bonnet."

He winked at me and I understood he'd let me stew in my own juices until I was good and ready to come out.

17

For the next few days, I stood at my window before dawn but Mr. Garibaldi didn't reappear.

At my regular breakfast with Harold, he told me about how he'd been born in England and was a manservant for lords and ladies, just like his father and father's father. When he first came to work for my Aunt, he lived above the garage, but moved into the main house to make room for me. His brother had an important position with the Coldstream Guards back in London.

Shopping with Harold had been quite an experience. First off, we went in the limo, which was too cool for words, to Worth Avenue, the ritzy shopping district. I felt a little guilty buying anything at all but there didn't seem to be a Wal-Mart handy and Harold never even looked at the price tags. He added my name to Aunt Rowena's account at Saks, The Purple Parrot and Neiman-Marcus.

I really needed new shoes and ended up with sandals, flip-flops and tennis shoes along with five matching shorts and halter outfits, a black satin running suit, jeans and a hooded sweatshirt. Oh, and a one-piece hot pink bathing suit.

Every day, around noon, I put on my bathing suit,

grabbed a towel, flip-flops, sun block, slipped on Marla's sunglasses and wandered down to the beach. I passed the pool on the way. It was quite remarkable, with a beautiful tile design of mermaids on the bottom. One simply walked down the tile steps at one end right into the water. There was no diving board because the water was only about four feet deep all the way across. It was built to be stared at rather than swum in.

I walked across the lawn in my bare feet. The grass was stiff and sharp, and by the time I reached the ocean, the soles of my feet were all tingly. (In Philly, there was only a narrow strip of lawn outside my apartment building, and it was filled with empty beer bottles and crumpled McDonald's bags.)

On the beach, I sat in a woven chair shaped like a seashell. First thing I'd do was push my feet into the hot sand until I couldn't stand it anymore and then wiggle my toes until I got to the cool, wet sand underneath.

The ocean was blue out where the yachts were anchored but dirty brown where it crashed into the beach. Seagulls hung like puppets above the waves, honking away. On shore, they'd strut about, pecking at the dead fish when they had a mind to. There was also a dock that extended out into the ocean like a skinny white finger.

While I sat on the beach all lathered up with lotion and

hidden behind my sunglasses, I thought about the mysterious Mr. Garibaldi. The fact that Harold knew nothing of his origins or what he was doing there only increased my curiosity. Was he a vampire or wasn't he? What strange hold did he have over Aunt Rowena, who wouldn't take in blood without a fight, let alone a stranger? Questions tumbled about in my head but there were no answers.

I thought I might see or hear something when I walked past the cottage. It had stucco walls and a clay tile roof, just like the main house. The front door had a rounded top and a lion's head with a knocker ring. Getting close to the windows was impossible because of the thick, pointy-leafed plants around the outer walls. In front was a shady flagstone patio with a cast-iron round table and chairs.

When the sun splashed the cottage, it seemed magical, something out of a fairy tale.

Other times, when the clouds came out and shade swallowed it—well, let's just say you could imagine all sorts of strange, dark happenings inside that cottage.

18

One day Harold told me I'd been on the estate long enough.

"I don't want you driving me around in the limo."

"I've a better idea. Come along."

He pushed open the doors to the garage. As you can imagine, it was like nothing I'd ever seen. Burgundy tile covered the floor, which sloped toward two circular drain grates in the middle. A brass showerhead sat above each of the cars. The walls were stucco. Along the back wall sat a tool bench filled with tools, neatly arranged, like silverware at the dinner table.

"What kind of cars are those?" I asked.

"The white one is a 1969 Mercedes 300 SEL. The fastest production sedan ever made. The silver one is a Rolls Royce Corniche. You are, of course, familiar with the limo."

The limo didn't do anything for me but the Mercedes and Rolls were a sight to behold.

Harold walked over to the wall where a bike hung on two hooks. He took it down and wheeled it over to me.

Clunky, with thick tires, fenders and colorful streamers coming out of the plastic handles, I thought I wouldn't be caught dead on that in my old neighborhood. Or anywhere.

"A Schwinn 'Phantom'. You can use it anytime you like. Best thing for you, a bracing bike ride before the evening meal. Work up an appetite, what? A nice routine is what you need."

Even though I thought the last thing I needed was a nice routine, I began to ride. Harold was right. The bike was a no-speed, so pedaling was excellent exercise. And it was good for me to get off the estate.

Harold gave me five dollars every morning at breakfast and told me to do with it what I wished. I asked if maybe I should get a job, but he frowned and said it wouldn't do to have Rowena Thibideaux's niece working.

Well, okay.

Riding gave me a better perspective. Aunt Rowena lived on South Ocean Boulevard, sort of the main drag, mansion-wise. Lake Worth separated Palm Beach from the mainland. Harold cautioned me I was not to leave the island itself, for there were areas where a "proper young lady should not venture unescorted." I would hardly consider myself proper, but I listened to him, nonetheless.

My usual routine was to ride along the Lake Trail. Paved and landscaped, it was created for bike riders and joggers. In a shady nook were water fountains and benches. I'd stop there and cool down for a bit before continuing on to Worth Avenue.

I was already familiar with Saks and Neiman Marcus due to my shopping expedition with Harold. Gucci and Luis Vuitton and Armani had stores here too, along with art galleries and such. Worth Avenue was so classy you bought eyeglasses at a place called 'Optique.'

I got into the habit of stopping at the Starbucks and

grabbing an iced caramel macchiato. There were tables with umbrellas on the sidewalk outside where I'd finish my drink while I watched the world go by.

When I returned home, I took a shower and went down for the dinner meal. At first, I ate in the dining room all by myself at an enormous table. I felt ridiculous, having Magda standing over me while I ate, whisking the plates away as soon as I finished. I finally asked Harold to join me.

"That would not be possible. I eat in the kitchen."

"I won't tell."

"It is out of the question."

"Then I'll eat in the kitchen with you."

Henceforth, Harold and I sat in the kitchen and ate three-course gourmet meals that Chaco prepared. We always started with a soup, sometimes cold like strawberry and sometimes hot, like black bean. The main course was broiled mahi-mahi or salmon, with thin green beans or squash and potatoes squeezed out into nice little florets. For desert, there was first a fruit sorbet, to cleanse our palate, as Harold explained, and a fancy torte or crème brulee.

"Chaco doesn't talk much," I noted one night.

Harold shrugged. Apparently, it didn't matter to him how much she did or didn't talk.

"What's Mr. Garibaldi's first name?"

"Antonio."

"I haven't seen him about lately. Are you sure he's okay? "

Harold didn't answer.

"I actually don't care about Mr. Garibaldi anyway," I said as though the subject was suddenly bothersome to me.

Fact was, after days of wondering about what went on inside the caretaker's cottage I decided to see for myself.

19

I've had three obsessions in my life.

For a five-year-old where apartments, towns and her mother's boyfriends changed with dizzying frequency, the world seemed an unsettled place at best. In the midst of this chaos the only constant, my one beacon of certainty, was the U.S. Mail. It arrived at different times in different places and the first thing I did when we moved into a new apartment was figure out the delivery schedule. I'd listen for the telltale scuff of the mailman walking up the steps and the slap of the mailbox door. Waiting until he disappeared—one mustn't appear too eager—I then retrieved my daily treasure.

"What's r-e-s-i-d-e-n-t mean?"

"It means the person who is living here."

"Us?"

"Us."

I was amazed the postal service knew where we were going to be before we did and took it as a certain sign that Gina Luginbill and her daughter Lila truly mattered in the scheme of things.

The highlight of my day was sorting the mail into neat piles. I saved every single piece of mail we received. Neatly sorted or not, it turned into serious clutter.

"We can't keep piles of mail, Lila. I don't mind you keeping some, but the rest of it has to go."

Mother found me a wicker basket and declared I could keep all the mail that fit inside. When I started school, I thought it strange that none of the other kids wanted to talk about their mail collections at lunch. In fact, no one else had one.

The world suggested by those envelopes was one filled with opportunities, ("Instant Winner!!") or pressing questions, (Bad Credit???). My teachers were less than pleased with my stylistic twist of adding multiple exclamation points and question marks when a single whatever would suffice.

I was particularly enthralled by the reply cards. They suggested a better life was only a return card away. Those were better off than Mother and I (and certainly there were such people) were that way because they were "Instant Winners!!!" I insisted Mother complete every reply card. ("We really are gonna win a ranch in New Mexico, Mother!!!"). I didn't know anything about probability and was absolutely certain the more cards we sent in the better chance we had of winning. I was doing my part in getting us out of our desperate straits, the least she could do was fill in the blanks and mail the cards.

We never won that ranch in New Mexico. We never won a single thing.

I was soon exhausted by a world that promised so much and delivered so little. Someone, not me, was an "Instant Winner!!!" and there was no need to "Hurry!!!" about anything at all. The reply cards were dispatched into the same distant, vague system that delivered them. I imagined an alternative world where other poor, rootless children received my completed reply cards as evidence the world cared.

Then, one day, Mother asked me to fetch the nail clippers from her bedroom. Now her bedroom always looked like a hurricane had just passed through, so I had to rummage about a bit. I moved a blouse from the dresser and a handful of cards fluttered to the floor. Incredulously, I realized that while Mother had certainly filled them out, she'd never mailed them. Why, that ranch in New Mexico card was at least a year old! She was so disorganized she couldn't even dispose of the evidence of her deception.

For a long time, I was madder than a hornet at Mother. The way I figured it, she should have refused the fill out the cards from the get-go, or having filled them out should have sent them, or not having sent them made sure I never found them. Eventually, my anger faded and the world seemed drearier. We were what we were, Mother and I, and nothing, it seemed, would ever change that.

It would be six years until, at the age of eleven, I was introduced to the subject of my next obsession. BLACK HOLES. (In those days certain words appeared as capital block letters on the billboard in my brain whenever I said them.) On a field trip to the planetarium, the guide explained that a BLACK HOLE was an extremely dense celestial body. The example she used was a marble weighing as much as the Earth. A marble weighing as much as the Earth! Fancy that! Who worried about such matters? Where were these people? Why didn't any of them live in my apartment building? Why didn't Mother date one of *them*?

Unlike the U.S. Mail's reassuring, humdrum regularity, even thinking about that VERY HEAVY MARBLE gave me a headache. What if a BLACK HOLE was dislodged in a way we'd never considered and raced toward Earth? You couldn't intercept it with fighter planes or missiles, because it was the size of a marble! When it hit the Earth it would be like two pool balls colliding and the Earth would make a beeline toward the side pocket that was the Sun and life, as we knew it, would end. The end of existence weighed heavy on my mind. Unexpected obliteration!!!

"Whatever are you talking about, Lila?"

"If a marble was a BLACK HOLE it would weigh as much as the Earth."

"A marble can't be a black hole and a black hole can't be a marble. So it doesn't matter what it weighs, does it?"

It was my lot in life to worry about theoretical physics as well as make out the weekly grocery list. Now I would have gladly done the shopping if I were Einstein's daughter but there was clearly no theoretical thinking going on inside Mother's brain.

Coincidentally (or not) my concern with the BLACK HOLE arrived about the time I started my period. My first day's cramps liked to bend me in two. Mother was understanding and let me stay home if I wanted to. While lying in bed with a wad of cotton between my legs soaking up blood that poured from my body because I was physically able to give birth years before I needed to, wanted to, or should, I took comfort in the fact that some aspect of existence was capable of explanation, in spite of my experience to date. Did a star turn into a BLACK HOLE years before it needed to? Well, of course it didn't!

The universe might be infinite and unforgiving, but at least it operated according to a strict set of rules. My obsession with black holes faded as I learned to tolerate my monthly cycle. All that remained was my fascination with the pure logic of mathematics, a good thing if you think about it. I didn't obsess about anything else until —

A. (I started referring to Antonio by a single letter, for no reason than it made him seem even more mysterious. In my mind, at least.)

Now the only thing the U.S. Mail, black holes and A. had in common is me, and I believe it was the natural rhythm of life that made certain I had a mystery to contemplate whenever I really needed one.

20

The key to the cottage was inside the security closet. I hung around the kitchen as Chaco prepared to leave for the day and Harold retired to his room. I had to leave the main house with Chaco. Thankfully, everything was so organized I just opened the door and removed the key when she ducked in the bathroom.

At nine o'clock that night A., appeared, dressed in his

tuxedo and trailing smoke. He strolled in the direction of the ocean.

I waited for nearly an hour before leaving my apartment. Just the hint of a breeze disturbed the hot night air as I crossed the courtyard.

During the day, the mansion reminded me of a slab of strawberry ice cream. When the sun went down, the mansion became a dark, hulking presence. The spotlights hidden in the bushes cast grotesque shadows against the foundation, suggesting misshapen creatures that only came out at night.

By the time I reached the front door of the cottage, my hands were drenched with sweat. I took a deep breath and tried to insert the key, only to find my hand shook as if I had the palsy. I knew what I was doing was wrong. Marla and Harold would be terribly disappointed to know what I was up to, but before I could pull the key out, the lock clicked and the door opened just a smidgen.

As I stood outside the door and debated whether I should chuck it all, an intriguing aroma of tobacco and leather seeped out of the door and tickled my nostrils. I was helpless to resist. I swallowed hard and entered.

I can recall every detail of that cottage. Rough-hewn wood beams supported the ceiling. The walls were stucco and the floor reddish clay tiles. Brass wall sconces were placed at regular intervals along the walls and cast yellow light upward. The windows were narrow and made of thick green glass. The combination of yellow light and green glass created the strange glow in the grove at night.

There were two other round-topped doors in the far wall of the room. I didn't have the nerve to peek inside. Besides, there was far too much to see in the main room.

A leather sofa and matching chair were grouped around a ponderous coffee table. To my left sat a tall wooden case with rows of cubbyholes. Inside each cubbyhole was a long roll of paper. I didn't dare to remove them. They felt old and fragile to the touch. A shelf above the cubbyholes held brass instruments I thought for certain were antique measuring devices. On a second shelf sat models of sailboats. A hump-backed travel trunk with leather straps rested behind the sofa.

On the coffee table was a collection of framed photographs. I had only seen him from a distance, but I knew these were pictures of Mr. Garibaldi as a younger man. He was quite handsome.

I have those pictures here with me but I don't have to look at them to recall the details: A., standing on a dock next to a hanging shark; on a rocky ridge surrounded by Aborigines; in a desert with camels and men wearing long black cloaks, their faces covered with black cloth. I think they were Bedouins or some such nomads.

One photo jumped out at me. At first I thought I was looking at myself, but then I realized the photo was of Aunt Rowena when she in her twenties.   Once again, I was struck by our physical similarities. Her photo solved one mystery. A. and Aunt Rowena had known each other in a past life.

On the other side of the room was a square table and on the table sat a map, the corners held down by brass weights. It wasn't like any map I'd ever seen, being crosshatched by lines and small numbers. In the center of the map were several islands, identified as the "Dry Tortugas."

The notion popped into my head that A. was a soldier-of-fortune who had traveled all over the world and now, as the final chapter of his career, was hot on the trail of buried treasure while hiding out in Aunt Rowena's estate.

It made more sense than believing he was a vampire; besides, he'd spent an awful lot of time in the sun during his youth, not the sort of behavior that's good for a vampire's health.

Just then, a chime went off that fair to stopped my heart. I screamed and my hand went up to my mouth. It was only a pendulum clock. My heart didn't stop palpitating for five minutes. No point in pushing my luck. As I turned to leave, I saw a pack of matches lying on the floor. The cover was hot pink and read "Club Coral."

I slipped them in my pocket. I returned to my apartment around midnight and shut the door behind me. My knees turned to jelly. I slid down into a heap. My heart pounded, my mouth was dry as sand and my hands were wet as sponges.

What I had done was wrong, pure and simple. I didn't do it to act out or prove a point or even steal anything. I did it because not all the stolen credit cards in the world could buy what I wanted.

From the moment I saw A. emerge from the mist I felt he was somehow related to my quest to determine where I fit into the larger scheme of things. And I was right!

Dry Tortugas.

Club Coral.

As mystifying as hieroglyphics revealed in the flickering light of an archeologist's torch, those four words were the key to unlocking A's past and, with a growing sense of certainty, my future.

21

The next morning I joined Harold for breakfast. After we finished eating, I helped him clear off the table.

"Remember when you said I should ask if I needed anything?"

"Indeed."

"Would it be too much trouble if I got a laptop? I know they're expensive—"

"I know nothing of such matters but Miss Rowena has engaged a consultant relative to technology."

He opened a drawer and removed a notebook and pen.

"Provide specifications of your requirements," he said.

I took the notebook and pen. "Would be okay if I asked for a MacBook?"

"Miss Lila, just write down what you need."

I wrote down a MacBook and printer and handed it back to him.

"And what about the Internet?"

"You have a data port in the apartment. Miss Rowena is quite an eBay devotee."

I went down to the beach around eleven. I returned at three to find two boxes and a bag sitting on my bed. One box held a MacBook and the other a small laser printer. Inside the bag were printer paper and numerous cables. Aunt Rowena certainly had the world at her beck-and-call.

When I had set everything up, I checked the Internet for

JAILBAIT.COM but the site was gone. I was relieved to learn my perfect little ass was no longer on display for the world to see.

I created an e-mail account and sent a message to Marla, telling her everything was fine and thanking her once again for her help. I also did a search to see if Mother had been arrested but 'Gina Luginbill' didn't turn up any matches.

I then checked for a 'Club Coral' website or listing but found neither.

I had already decided not to go to the cottage every night. Rule was, I couldn't return unless I unraveled at least one mystery encountered on the previous visit. Having struck out on the Club Coral, I turned to the Dry Tortugas.

They are a cluster of islands located about seventy miles west of the Florida Keys, discovered by Ponce De Leon in 1513. He named them the "Tortugas" after the sea turtles that lived there, but later "dry" was added to the map so people knew there was no fresh water on the islands. (I wondered if there was such a thing as the "Wet Tortugas" but could not find any reference to them.)

Fort Jefferson was located on one of the islands. It was built to protect southern shipping lanes and later used as a Union prison during the Civil War. I wondered whether Buford Thibideaux had spent time there before being hung from his yardarm.

The map with all the numbers and strange lines? It was a navigational chart. I wondered if A. intended to sail there himself, no mean feat. The islands were just a few little smidgens of land in the middle of the ocean. If you missed them, you might sail all the way to Mexico. I looked up some information on navigation and to my delight learned it had an awful lot to do with mathematics. For instance, Dead Reckoning, by which you estimate your position based on your course and known speed, requires the ability to make a TSD (time-speed-distance) calculation.

I had never thought about sailing once in my entire life and I was entangled in navigational charts and TSD calculations. But that's what obsession is all about, isn't it? Anyway, having solved one mystery, per my rule, I was now free to return to the cottage.

I did so three days later. This time my mystery consisted of two bound volumes I found on one of the bookcases. The cover page of the first read: "The Competition. A Screenplay by W. Tyler Calderone. Property of National Picture Corporation." The other, "Amorous," also belonged to National Pictures.

On and off over the next week I tried to figure why A. would have screenplays in his cottage. I couldn't find a single word about W. Tyler Calderone on the Internet. Neither movie was available on video.

I suppose most seventeen-year-olds might have found this all terribly boring. I had no idea what Lady Gaga was up to, no need to hang out at the mall to meet boys, no concern over the color of my hair or the size of my breasts. Such matters were trivial beyond belief to me now. The night I spent crying myself to sleep when I first arrived seemed a lifetime ago. Mother's betrayal was now a scab on my heart I had no intention of picking.

There are many ways to express what I felt during those few short weeks after I arrived: I had stumbled onto an alternative reality I could never find again if I left, or I was in the midst of a dream that would vanish forever when I woke, or (I imagined Aunt Rowena thinking) I was a parasite that would perish if detached from its host.

I was one with 'Sea Spray,' the protectiveness of Harold and the delicate mystery that was A. It was unthinkable that I would ever leave.

22

"Excuse me, Miss Lila, but I have terrible news."

"It's my mother, isn't it? She and Luther got ambushed on some country road and I must go and identify her bullet-riddled body." The last scene from *Bonnie and Clyde* played inside my head.

It was seven o'clock in the morning. Harold stood in the doorway of my apartment, hands folded against his tummy, head slightly bowed.

"Oh, gracious no. It is, I fear, my brother. He has suffered a stroke. I must return to forthwith to England. I'm so very sorry."

Why was Harold apologizing to me when his brother had a stroke? He cleared his throat and looked away.

"What is it?"

"Miss Lila, would that I could change circumstances, but without my presence you cannot remain."

The air went out of my lungs as though someone punctured a balloon with a pin.

"I have already contacted Ms. Johnson and have made the necessary arrangements for your return."

"How long will you be gone?" It almost hurt to talk.

"At least two weeks, perhaps longer."

"I can take care of myself for that long. I promise I won't get into trouble."

He stiffened. "Miss Rowena has made herself clear on this matter. Since the date of my return is indeterminate, you cannot remain. I'm so terribly sorry."

I stood there in the doorway and watched him walk down the steps. I was paralyzed but I did my best thinking in stressful situations.

I caught up with him before he was halfway across the courtyard.

"Harold, if Mr. Garibaldi agreed to watch after me, could I stay?"

"There is not a scintilla of a chance he would agree to such an arrangement."

"But if he did?"

Harold turned back, a sly smile on his face. "Aren't we the cheeky one? You must ask him yourself and resolve this before the morrow. If he agrees, I shall make it right with Miss Rowena. Otherwise, we shall leave for the airport at noon."

23

I rode the bike down to Saks and charged a black dress, one that would not expose the swell of my breasts or hug the curves of my perfect little ass. I wanted A. to think of me as someone who couldn't possibly cause any trouble. I also picked up a pair of very plain reading glasses, you know, to give me a studious appearance.

The idea that A. would take care of me was ridiculous,

but I wasn't going to leave Palm Beach without a fight.

At four a.m., I dragged myself out of bed and into the bath. I didn't wear any make up and pulled my hair back in a librarian bun. The reading glasses had the desired effect. I appeared quite studious and boring and, therefore, well behaved.

I waited outside the cottage and rehearsed what I was going to say. Very calm, very logical, so incredibly poised he wouldn't think twice about granting my request.

When he came strolling out of the mist around dawn, I started talking.

"Mr. Garibaldi, my name is Lila Thibideaux, of the Louisiana Thibideaux? I'm currently staying in the apartment over the garage and but since Harold has to go tend to his brother, who has a very important post with the Coldstream Guards back in England and has suffered a debilitating stroke, long – story - short if you don't agree to be responsible for me while he, speaking of Harold, is in England then I must go to home to Philadelphia, where, since my mother and her boyfriend are fugitives from a federal arrest warrant, I will be screamed at by a man wearing a dog collar."

Or something to that effect. Not at all what I had practiced. The words tumbled out of my mouth, try as I might to slow down.

He studied me for a long moment, walked into the cottage and shut the door.

Well, I never!

I used the ring in the mouth of the lion to let him know I was still waiting. He didn't answer so I rapped again. Finally, the door opened a crack.

"I don't think you understand the dire straits I find myself in. I simply cannot go back home. I will be put into a foster home and will surely find my way down the road to ruin. You don't want to be responsible for that, do you?"

He shut the door again.

I can recognize alcohol on the breath. I was dealing with a man under the influence and this was going to be an uphill battle. I rapped on the door again.

This time he swung the door open and stood with one hand on the doorframe, the other holding a martini glass. "Barthelme once used a single sentence to tell an entire story, a feat you have duplicated, unwittingly I am certain, although your breathless style does suggest a genuine lack of guile," he said in a butter-smooth voice just above a whisper.

I had no idea what he was talking about. "Let me start over. I'm—"

"Lila Thibideaux, of the Louisiana Thibideaux. Proceed."

"My mother abandoned me and Aunt Rowena took me in. My father was her brother. Aunt's Rowena's, that is."

"Do you have a cold?"

"It's my natural speaking voice."

"I see. Your accent tells me you were raised in the South. Not the Deep South, for you lack the requisite molasses-drenched drawl. Arkansas or Texas, I would guess. How old are you?"

"I'll be eighteen on September eighteenth."

He arched an eyebrow and sucked smoke from his cigarette, drawing it deep into his lungs.

"If you agree to be responsible for me until Harold returns from England, I can stay. It will only be for two weeks. I won't be a bit of trouble. Anyway, you're out all night but I don't do anything at night myself. You can lock me in my apartment when you leave and let me out when you get home."

He stared at a spot just to the right of my head for a long time and then back at me. "Your tale of woe, Dickensian in scale, along with your gamine charm, tugs at my heartstrings, but I have a rule that has served in good stead during my life."

"What's that?"

"I never agree to do something I have no intention of

doing." The door shut in my face.

I'd lost.

I was steaming mad at his rudeness. Wound tighter than a pocket watch and unable to sleep, I fired up the computer and used an on-line dictionary to look up some of the words he used. The word *gamine*, for instance, meant "street urchin." What was so charming about an urchin? One of the alternative definitions was "tomboy." There was a picture of someone named Twiggy next to the entry. I was insulted. I had curves where curves were supposed to be!

Barthelme (Donald) turned out to be a writer known for short-fiction. He also wrote a novel titled *Snow White*.

Guile meant "deviousness."

Before I could continue, there was a knock at my door. It was A. He took a step back when I opened the door, so we talked through the screen.

"How do you know what I do at night?"

I swallowed hard. "Why, whatever do you mean?"

"You said I was out all night. How would you know that?"

I felt my cheeks go hot. "Harold said you slept all day so I just figured—"

He didn't pursue it. "Who is the man in the dog collar?"

"It's just this way I have of thinking about how bad life would be if I was sent back to the shelter. You know, for abandoned girls."

"What does the man in the dog collar do?"

"There's not really a man in a dog collar, you understand."

"Humor me."

"He cracks a whip inside a boiler room and we all walk along in dirty dresses and stringy wet hair. There's lots of steam and clanging."

A. walked down the steps without saying another word. I can tell you I did not intend to grovel any further before Mr. Antonio Garibaldi. As far as I was concerned, he could go straight to hell in a hand basket!

My situation was one of those half-full, half-empty scenarios. I was going back to the shelter, but had a few weeks of grand living. I retrieved my diamond pendant and slipped it on.

I packed my bag, taking only back to Philadelphia what I brought with me. I set the alarm, then tossed and turned until the alarm woke me at eleven. I grabbed my bag and walked down to the courtyard, where a black limo idled.

Harold appeared, dressed in a blue suit. The limo driver loaded two leather suitcases into the trunk.

"Good morning, Lila." Harold checked his ticket and passport. "I think all is in order. Now then, I hope my return finds you hale and hearty." He handed me a roll of cash. "An advance on your pocket money."

"I'm staying?"

He slid into the rear seat. "I distinctly remember agreeing that if Mr. Garibaldi assumed responsibility for your well-being you could stay."

He waved at me from behind the window glass as the car pulled away. He had the oddest smile on his face, like the cat that swallowed the canary, if you catch my drift.

Even today, I have no way of explaining my total and absolute surprise. I stood in the courtyard for the longest time before I could take a step, as though in a dream, and if I moved, I would wake up and find myself in Philly again.

The lights were off in A's cottage. I was exhausted, so thanking A. personally would have to wait until I got some sleep.

24

Later that same day, a miserable rain swept across the estate.

Having struck out on the matter of Club Coral, I turned my attention to W. Tyler Calderone. It took a while but I happened across a site called "Hollywood's Greatest Scandals."

Everett Townsend, described as "haggard and ascetic", was heir to a ceramic plumbing fixture fortune. He married Ethel Coverdale, heir to a tobacco fortune.

Townsend bought National Pictures Corporation and moved to Hollywood. Ethel stayed back in New York. In 1970, National released a movie titled, *The Competitors*, about two brothers who ended up fighting on opposite sides of the Spanish Civil War. They both fell in love with the same woman. The actress who played this woman isn't important but there was another actress in the movie named Katherine Doubet, who played a bit part. The article didn't mention the writer of the movie but we all know it was W. Tyler Calderone.

Townsend, who was fifty and looked like he had a perpetual stomachache, was infatuated with Katherine. She was twenty-three. A "striking brunette with a come-hither look." The Hollywood press called them "Beauty and the Beast." Back in New York, Ethel filed for divorce.

National Pictures next movie was *Amorous* and this time Katherine was going to star. The plot was about two brothers who were pearl divers and fell in love with the same woman.

Townsend was up to his chin in creditors (eventually he sold his motion picture company to Republic Pictures). Word got back to Townsend that Katherine's kisses looked a little too real and she was cavorting about at night with one or both or her co-stars. He was apparently unwilling or unable to visit the location on the Baja Peninsula to do anything about that.

Townsend and Katherine eventually made up, or so it seemed. A few months later, at a party on Townsend's yacht, he and Katherine both ended up dead in his stateroom. The police ruled it a murder-suicide; that is, he shot her and then turned the gun on himself.

25

The skies cleared after the rain ended. I slipped on my bathing suit and wandered down to the beach, passing close by the cottage. I had a notion to knock on the door and thank A. but decided it was only noon and he was probably asleep.

I mostly wasted the rest of the day at the beach, had dinner by myself and went back to my room.

In spite of my upbringing I was, in many ways, a very responsible person. I guess that comes from having to take care of Mother in various and sundry matters as previously discussed.

While it is true that some days I could be a hellion if the mood struck, deep down, I believed I was solid as the day is long.

This explains why, after two days of waiting, I decided to

take matters into my own hands and find out exactly what A. expected of me.

I waited for him outside his cottage the next morning. It was before dawn and soon enough he came strolling up with his tuxedo jacket slung over his shoulder.

"Hi," I said, casual as could be.

He grunted so I knew he heard me but didn't slow down. He entered his cottage and shut the door.

I banged the lion's head ring and waited.

A few minutes passed. I banged again. The door finally opened a crack. He had taken off his tuxedo shirt and wore what we called a 'wife-beater T-shirt' on Philly but, as I later learned, was properly termed a 'singlet.'

"I just wanted to thank you for agreeing to take care of me and wondered if you had any rules for me to follow."

He opened his mouth to reply but then slumped against the door. He started to slide down and I grabbed hold of him.

"Put your arm over my shoulder," I said.

I dragged him into the cottage and laid him down on the leather couch.

"Are you okay?"

He motioned me away. "I'm fine," he said softly.

"You ought to lie still for a while," I offered, taking a seat.

"Good thing I was around, huh?"

He didn't respond.

"Maybe you should drink some water. Or take an aspirin. I could call a doctor."

He looked directly at me. "Do you really want to be helpful?"

"Yes."

"Then shut up."

I sat on the leather chair opposite the couch and waited. I think he fell asleep on and off. We sat there in silence, he on the couch and I on the chair, until sunlight seeped through the windows.

Finally, he sat up.

"Bring me my jacket."

His tuxedo jacket was lying across the desk. I brought it to him. He fished out a silver cigarette case and Zippo lighter.

"I don't think you should be smoking."

He lit the cigarette anyway. "Now then, exactly why were you skulking about outside my door?"

"I wanted to thank you for agreeing to take care of me for the next two weeks."

"I agreed to nothing of the sort."

"Harold said you did."

He glanced at his watch. "It's six-thirty. Come back at eight."

"Sure I can't do anything for you?"

He stood and walked away. He waved his hand in my direction, shooing me away, then entered the bathroom and shut the door.

I wondered if maybe he'd had one of those small strokes and had forgotten what he told Harold. I doubted that Harold had made it all up, considering how insistent he was that he couldn't leave me alone at Sea Spray.

The other option was that A. had changed his mind, but he didn't seem the sort who changed his mind very often. He was set in his ways, best I could tell.

I returned at the appointed time. A. opened the door and walked away. I didn't go in right away because I was struck with the notion that this was the first time he'd invited me in. The entire vampire thing raised its ugly head again. You know, "enter freely of your own will" and all that.

I went inside anyway. I figured that even if he was a vampire and decided to take care of me, I'd get to stay on the estate *and* live forever, so what did I have to lose?

He'd set a small round table with glasses for water and orange juice, silverware and cloth napkins.

He appeared a moment later carrying a single plate holding a perfect omelet, what with little brown patches here and there and all in one piece. There were also English muffins and jams.

"Aren't you eating?" I asked but he went back into what I assumed was the kitchen. After a few moments, I heard the telltale sound of an espresso machine. He appeared carrying two tiny cups on saucers.

"I've already eaten," he continued without skipping a beat.

Up until that moment, every time I was in A's presence it was either dark or I was obsessed with getting my words out or helping him when he fainted and so I hadn't really taken in his appearance.

He wore a black polo shirt, gray linen pants, and black leather loafers. He was on the short side of six feet but not by much. Trim and fit, he had a broad chest and shoulders that implied he was stronger than you might guess at first glance. His arms were toned, like the rowers I sometimes watched on the Schuylkill River back in Philly.

He moved gracefully, without a lot of wasted motion. Compared to Luther, who I saw as a big, unruly dog, A. had an effortless elegance to his movements akin to a panther.

His silver hair was cut short. Not severely, like a jarhead, but just long enough to require a comb to keep it groomed. His jaw was square and his neatly trimmed gray moustache accented his thin lips.

His complexion was olive, as befitted his obvious Italian heritage. The gaze from his steely blue eyes was direct and unrelenting.

There was no denying he was an attractive man. An attractive *older* man, that is, because although he was aging well he was clearly aging. A spider web of lines surrounded his eyes. The skin on his neck was loose. There were age spots on the back of his hands.

"Something on your mind?" he asked and I realized I was gawking at him.

As I ate, he lit another cigarette and sipped his coffee.

"This is a surprisingly good omelet."

"Surprisingly?"

"It's just that most of the men I know can't boil water."

"What men?"

"My mother's boyfriends."

"How many has she had?"

"Oh," I said, pushing away the empty plate, "let's see." I added them up in my head. "Fifteen, give or take."

I took a sugar cube from a dish and dropped it into the espresso. I sipped it and screwed up my face because it was much stronger than an iced caramel macchiato. I dropped in two more sugar cubes.

"Let us be perfectly clear on one point. I did not tell Harold I would assume responsibility for your well-being."

"You didn't? Did he talk to you about it?"

"No."

I harrumphed and crossed my arms over my chest. "Not that I don't believe you, but I can't imagine why he would say so if it wasn't true."

"I have no idea. Let us consider our situation. According to your account, if I do not agree you will be sent back to Philadelphia and the man in the dog collar."

"There's not a man in a dog collar. I just—"

He waved his hand, chasing my protest away. "Whether or not I agreed, you have escaped banishment. I'm certain Harold had his reasons for granting you a reprieve."

"I suppose so."

"I assume you will keep out of trouble for the next two weeks?"

"Yes sir, I can."

"You mean, you will."

"Yes, sir."

"Do not leave the estate after dark."

I nodded.

"I do not expect to be bothered by the local gendarmes concerning your activities. If they show up at my door wondering why you were caught shoplifting I will tell them I have never seen you before and you are not a resident of this estate."

"I'm not going to shoplift," I said with a little snap in my voice. "I am not some poor white trash *gamine*, I'll have you know."

Just the hint of a smile crossed his face. "Then we understand each other?"

"Completely."

"Good. I expect this is the last time you will darken my door."

You know, there was just something in his tone that really pissed me off. "Fine," I said. "But the next time you faint in your doorway don't think I'll be around to help you."

He studied me through a haze of cigarette smoke.

"And those things are going to kill you," I said.

By the time I got back to my apartment, I'd cooled down. What did it matter if I saw him again anyway? In two weeks

Harold would be return, life would return to normal, and Mr. Antonio Garibaldi could keep doing whatever he did at night.

26

I stayed away from A.'s cottage, not even bothering to go down to the beach.

About two days later a heat wave hit, and I mean it was *hot*, at least one hundred in the shade. When I stepped outside the heat took my breath away. I slept on and off during the day. It was too hot to ride my bike into town.

At night, it cooled down a bit, but there wasn't even a hint of an ocean breeze.

On the second night, I pulled on my bathing suit and went for a swim in the pool. It was weird, swimming in the dark, but it did serve to cut the heat. After splashing about for a while, I hung on the side and peered at the cottage.

In spite of my snit over his attitude, the time I spent with A. only whetted my appetite to learn more about him. Since I wasn't going to be interacting with him again, I decided to observe him from afar in an organized manner.

Back in the apartment, I fired up the laptop and made up a spreadsheet. Then I set the clock for four a.m.

As it turned out, he had an irregular schedule. I thought he wore the tuxedo every night, but on Monday, Tuesday and

Wednesday nights he left around nine wearing a pair of painter's pants and a blue work shirt. He wouldn't return at all on those days until nearly nine the next morning. He wore the tuxedo on Thursday, Friday and Saturday, left around nine and returned at four a.m. I never saw him leave or return on a Sunday.

Clearly, the next step in my surveillance was to follow him.

I waited in the shadows beneath the steps to my apartment. When he departed wearing his tuxedo, I followed him toward the ocean and watched as a small motor launch pulled up to the dock. He got on and headed north. I watched until the darkness swallowed the running lights.

There being no way I could follow the launch, I decided where he went in his tuxedo would remain a mystery.

On Tuesday night, he stood at the top of the driveway. After a few moments, an old red pickup appeared and he got in.

I couldn't follow him on the ocean but I certainly could follow him on land. In order to do so I had to break my promise not to leave the estate at night. I thought about it for a bit and then decided it was only for one night and an essential part of my research.

The next night he was scheduled for his truck ride I sat on my bike far enough down the street so he couldn't possibly see me.

No one was ever on the street after dark. Even during the day, only a few cars passed. The most activity was in the morning and between five and six when the maids and gardeners left for the day.

I followed at a discrete distance through the town until the truck swerved down a narrow road along the beach and we entered the Palm Beach City Marina. Yachts and enormous powerboats bobbed next to the many docks. Music floated in the night air and giggling girls in bikinis seemed to be everywhere.

I kept pedaling and soon the sounds of the parties faded, replaced by smaller boats on trailers and a row of what looked like warehouses.

The truck pulled to a stop in front of a warehouse surrounded by a chain link fence. I watched a black man get out and unlock the gate. The truck pulled in and A. got out. The black man then unlocked the warehouse door and they both went inside.

Just as I was ready to move closer a dog came out of nowhere, slamming against the chain metal fence next to me, barking furiously. I nearly swallowed my heart!

I turned around and pedaled out of there as fast as I could, hoping that A. wouldn't walk out of the warehouse to see what the commotion was all about.

I found my way back to Ocean Boulevard but hadn't gone twenty yards when a police cruiser pulled up next to me.

The policeman got out. He was a beefy guy but had a friendly face.

"You live around here?"

"Sea Spray."

"Ms. Thibideaux's place?"

"Yes, sir. I'm Lila Thibideaux, her niece. I'm staying there for the summer."

He nodded. "Have any identification?"

"No sir, it's back at the apartment. I stay above the garage."

"You do."

I had the distinct feeling he didn't believe me.

"Miss Thibideaux is away right now, if I recall. Always leaves for the summer. Who's there with you?"

"Harold, her manservant."

I felt a little flutter in my stomach. What if Harold told the police he was leaving?

"Actually, he's gone now. He had to go back to England."

"So you're staying there alone?"

"No. Mr. Garibaldi is looking over me. He's an old family

friend who's living in the caretaker's cottage."

The cop stared at me for a long time then tipped his cap. "I'll follow you back, just to make sure you get there safe and sound."

"I'd appreciate that, sir."

He got back into the cruiser and I started pedaling again. He followed a few feet behind. I used the keypad to open the front gate, then turned and waved at him. He waved back and drove off.

Back in my apartment I took a deep breath when I realized how close I'd come to screwing up. Sure, the cop believed me but what if he had a bad day himself and insisted on talking to A. to determine if my story was true? I would have no one to blame but myself for the consequences.

I had discovered where A. spent at least some of his nights, though I had no idea what he did inside the warehouse. I decided I would not push my luck in the future, because learning what A. did or did not do would not compensate for being sent back to Philly.

27

Remember my going on about how your life could be shrouded in the mist, and your biggest problem was walking into a door?

Sometimes when you least expect it, that's exactly what

happens.

The day started well enough. I retraced the route from the night before. The row of yachts was quiet, although I passed a woman in a bikini walking slowly toward the main street, yawning and obviously hung over.

I stayed far away from the chain link fences, on the ocean side. There was all sort of activity in the warehouses, sparks spraying and metal banging.

The pickup was gone but on the fence was a battered sign that read "Bill's Boats."

It was only ten in the morning so I decided to head up to the bike path. I rode about for a bit before stopping at the water fountain. I sat on a bench beneath the spreading branches of a large tree, closed my eyes and listened to the sound of the ocean.

I heard the sound of footsteps on the gravel and suddenly felt a body sit very close to me.

"Hello Lila."

My eyes snapped open. Sitting next to me was Luther Henderson.

"Don't do anything stupid," he said.

He'd changed his appearance, not surprising since he was on the lam. His head was bald as a cue ball. He'd grown a mustache and goatee. He wore a muscle shirt, a pair of plaid shorts and tennis shoes without socks. With his Wayfarer sunglasses, he projected a certain Bruce-Willis-Gone-Beach-Bum look.

He lifted his sunglasses. "Look-it here. Got you a perfect tan and everything. Living high on the hog over there at Sea Spray, like some highfalutin' society bitch."

"How do you know where I'm living?"

"This is Luther you're talking to. Finding you weren't any problem at all. Watching you was a bit harder but I must say your perfect little ass looks mighty fine in your hot pink bathing suit."

The thought of him watching made me sick to my stomach.

"Where's my mother?"

"She's fine. She wants to see you."

"Why didn't she come?

"She didn't know how you'd take the idea of seeing her again."

"I don't want to see her." I honestly didn't know how I felt about the idea.

Luther pushed his shoulder against mine.

"I think you better see her."

"Like I care what you think."

"Tomorrow, right here. Three o'clock." He stood and stretched. "And don't go thinking about running to the police."

"Why shouldn't I?"

"Because you don't want to be the one who puts your mother in stir, that's why."

He disappeared into the bushes.

Who the hell did Mother think she was! She didn't have the decency to show her face, sending her Bruce-Willis-Beach-Bum instead! She was the reason I had to leave Philadelphia! (I was better off in Palm Beach, but you catch my drift.)

By the time I stopped at Starbucks for my iced caramel macchiato, I was fairly steaming! I sat inside and stared at the floor for the longest time but gradually calmed down.

How did I know Luther was telling the truth? All sorts of scenarios flashed through my mind: Mother's dismembered body lying in the Everglades; or having just taken a pee in a filthy gas station, she steps into the west Texas sun in time to see Luther driving off in a cloud of dust; or she slaps Luther across the face and stomps off, finally fed up with his utter stupidity in the face of life.

I reached the end of my drink and the slurping woke me from my reverie. Gradually, I felt my pulse quicken at the prospect of seeing her.

Next day I showed up and waited. Mother didn't show up, but Luther did.

"Where's Mother?" I asked.

He glanced around. "Let's just say we were checking to see whether or not you could be trusted."

"Mother doesn't trust me? Is that it?"

"Folks in our situation can't be too careful," Luther replied. "Tomorrow morning. Nine o'clock."

"What if I don't want to spend my day waiting around for you and Mother?"

His eyes went cold and lifeless and for the first time I understood that within Luther did beat a true heart of darkness.

28

Next day, I waited until ten and rode my bike for a while, returning at noon. They didn't show then either. I had no desire to continue riding about aimlessly so I returned to the estate.

I returned at three and waited until four. Just as I was about to leave, Mother called to me from the bushes behind the bench. She stepped into view.

Her hair was jet-black and spiky short. She wore sunglasses. In her faded blue jeans, shapeless flowered blouse and ratty tennis shoes she was in real desperado mode.

You might think the first thing we'd do is hug, but we

never were very touchy-feely. Mother once said she had Scandinavian blood somewhere in her past and apparently they don't touch each other except for sex.

She motioned for me to join her. We walked along the path toward the waterway.

Normally, her skin gave off this healthy glow, but it had turned ashen and oily. I had the terrible thought that she was dying of some incurable disease.

"Are you sick, Mother? Are you dying?"

"I ain't dying, child."

"Take off your sunglasses, Mother. I want to see your eyes." She stopped and slid up her sunglasses, visor-like. Mother could cry for days, on and off, over her latest failed romance. Frankly, it didn't look like she cried a drop since she abandoned her only daughter.

"It took forever to find you, honey."

"Why didn't you just stop at the public welfare department and ask them where I was?"

"I'm sorry about Luther and me leaving you behind, but we have been unfairly accused."

"Then hire a lawyer."

"We don't have any money for a lawyer, least not one who could take on the F.B.I. That's why we need your help."

"You want my help, ditch Luther."

She stopped and stared across the water. "That's frankly out of the question. Luther helped me see the light of day, particularly as regards the circumstances of your conception."

"Luther is an idiot."

She pulled a yellowed piece of paper from her purse and thrust it at me.

"This is your birth certificate, child! It is signed by Denton Thibideaux. You are the rightful heir to Denton's fortune!" She spoke insistently, even though she couldn't raise her voice above a whisper for fear of drawing attention.

"Mother, we already know that dog won't hunt."

"If you grew up and became President of the United States, you can bet the Thibideaux clan would come out of the woodwork to get tickets to your inauguration. The Thibideaux seed sprouted within my garden. My flesh and its flesh became one. I will not be denied!"

I had never heard Mother speak with such conviction. She was using Luther's words, of course, what with seeds sprouting in a garden and turning to flesh like some *Invasion of the Body Snatchers* scenario. Leave it to Luther to mix metaphors.

"Your flesh is going to prison, Mother."

She glanced around quickly then stepped closer. "We

need you to turn off the alarm system to that pink house."

It took a few seconds for this all to register. They wanted me to help them burgle Sea Spray!

"One hour, honey. We will be in and out. You've got to help me with this, honey." She was dead serious.

"Well, I'm not there alone. There's a butler."

"You think Luther doesn't know you are there all alone at night?"

I had no way to know how Luther knew that, but he obviously did.

"No way, Mother."

She grabbed me by the arm. "Think about the life you led all because the Thibideaux clan refused to live up to their responsibilities!"

"What does any of that have to do with stealing from Aunt Rowena?"

"For all you know, Aunt Rowena inherited that pink house from Denton. That house is rightfully yours!"

A half-laugh escaped my lips. I walked in a tight circle, approximating the direction the conversation was headed. Mother was living proof a person could rationalize just about anything in their life, if they had a mind to.

"Let me get this straight. This wouldn't be stealing,

because the house might be mine after all?"

After a moment, Mother replied, "Well, yes."

As I said many times, Mother was not the sharpest knife in the drawer. She fumbled in her raggedy purse for her cigarettes, lit one and blew a stream of smoke into the air. She tapped her right toe furiously.

"I am not going to stand here and argue. You are going to as you're told, Lila Valentine Thibideaux!"

The dreaded first-middle-last name command! In my entire life, she'd used it four times, max. She had definitely dug in her heels on this issue.

"I'll give you the diamond necklace, Mother. And I have some cash. I think you should take it and be on your way."

"Nobody asked your opinion, honey and don't take that personal."

"What exactly am I supposed to say when the police come?"

"We'll tie you up so it looks like strangers done you in. Luther has already cased out the place. You need to leave that front gate open and shut down the security system to the house. Luther has all the police patrols timed and everything. This ain't gonna affect you at all. Now, we are talking about tonight at three-thirty a.m." She stubbed out her cigarette. "And if you do not do this, then you are no blood of mine."

She flounced off as though we were both in fourth grade and she had just won an argument about which of us some boy liked better.

Blood.

I was sick of its very mention. Mother had set forth the proposition that because I was fathered by a Thibideaux I had a legitimate claim on any or all of the Thibideaux fortune and I should help steal some of this fortune from one Thibideaux in particular, Aunt Rowena, who had taken me in only because of a sense of duty to the Thibideaux bloodline *after* Mother had abandoned me in favor of someone who wasn't *blood*.

I rode my bike in a daze, only dimly aware of my legs pedaling. The further I rode, the more I understood Mother's fuzzy logic. If Denton married Mother, my life would have been different from the get-go. I would have attended private schools and been introduced to proper society at some fancy ball, dated boys with Roman numerals after their names and gone off to some swanky Southern girls' college and married very well, thank you.

However, Denton never created a legal relationship with Mother. And as she well knew, you were either married or you weren't. She didn't have a leg to stand on.

By virtue of signing my birth certificate, Denton admitted he'd fathered me. Incontrovertible evidence, as I figured it. I was indeed his daughter but we had no chance of winning that lawsuit with those thick-as-thieves judges.

The light Luther had helped Mother see was if the courts would not give me my due, we should just take it. Another great idea brought to you by The Idea Man.

He was using Mother, in a different way than Denton had, but using her just the same. Was there any doubt he'd dump her first chance he got?

Mother was going about this ass-backwards. The first thing she needed to do was face up to the federal warrant. She could turn state's evidence and leave Luther holding the bag.

I mean, this was such an open-and-shut case even I could argue it.

"Your Honor, the court has heard testimony that the Defendant, Gina C. Luginbill, never possessed a computer in her life. Moreover, prior to meeting Luther Henderson, she had never even logged onto the Internet. After Jailbait.Com went up, she never visited it because Mr. Henderson forbade her to touch the computer! She was an unwitting participant in his dastardly scheme. It is true that she used stolen credit card numbers to steal a gazillion dollars, but she relied upon Mr. Henderson's assurance that the business was going so well they were approved for forty-two new credit cards! Never mind that each credit card had a different name, your Honor, for you can see that love had truly made her blind."

By the time I reached Sea Spray I recognized it was my mission in life to save my mother—not from the F.B.I., or Luther Henderson or Earl T. Scomes.

But from herself.

29

There was one problem with Luther's plan. While I had the key to my apartment and the keypad combination to the front gate, I didn't have the code to the main house security system. I could get it easy enough but I didn't have it at the moment I returned to the estate.

I sat at the computer and compiled two lists on the issue of helping Mother burgle Sea Spray.

Should

1. She is my mother and told me to do this.

2. Denton was my father.

3. My rightful claim to the Thibideaux fortune would not stand in St. Charles Parish.

4. Everything is insured (probably.)

Shouldn't

1. Aunt Rowena had taken me in during my hour of need.

2. Harold would be very disappointed.

3. Marla would be very disappointed.

4. A. would be disappointed.

5. By helping Mother, I was helping Luther.

6. It was plain wrong, notwithstanding #3 under "Should."

The question boiled down to whether or not I wanted to disappoint the four people who had helped me in order to please the one person who had abandoned me.

The longer I stared at the list, the more I recognized how Luther was using the matter of my inheritance to steer Mother wrong. Left to her own devices, she would have simply talked about "the inheritance" and how life would have been different except for the thieves in St. Charles parish. Like her need to be a movie star, it would be a subject to raise wistfully now and again.

What if Luther was wrong about what was rightfully mine? I figured he knew as much about inheritance law in Louisiana as he did about affirmative action. I didn't even know if there was a law governing such matters, but it was easy enough to find out.

I typed "Louisiana law" into the search engine and ran off about fifty pages of stuff on what was termed "the rights of succession" in Denton's state of birth.

The matter of my inheritance was more complicated than either Luther or Mother realized.

Since I was under twenty-four, Louisiana law considered me a "forced heir" whether or not I was in the will. I had to inherit *something*. Of course, I could inherit something only if there *was* something to inherit. (That's not the law speaking. That's just common sense.)

Aunt Rowena said her father had chased his son out of the state and set up a trust fund to support him. From what I understood reading up on trusts, Denton didn't technically own the trust. That's why the trust was set up in the first place, to keep the money out of Denton II's hands. It probably ceased to exist when Denton met his bad end.

I remembered how Tom Cruise couldn't get his hands on the trust fund set up for Dustin Hoffman in *Rain Man* no matter what he did. You'd think Mother could have connected the dots on this one.

Should I have been upset about the fact I had no case against the Thibideaux clan? Maybe, but considering I'd never been rich it didn't seem to matter anyway.

I did not intend to open the house for Luther, but rather to confront Mother with the truth of our legal position. As the old saying goes, the truth shall set you free.

I could have called the police and set up a sting. Of course, Mother would have gone directly to jail and I didn't want that to happen. Not by my hand, at least.

I wanted to talk to A. about this problem. He'd made it clear he did not want to be involved in my life in any way. Bottom line? This was something I had to do all by myself.

I walked over to the kitchen and made small talk with Chaco. I asked her if anyone had called asking if my Aunt was home. She said there had been several calls but she told them my Aunt was gone for the summer. One or more of those calls had to be from Luther. He'd been watching me so he undoubtedly knew when Chaco and Magda left each day.

It seemed like forever until Chaco went to the bathroom. I slipped into the security closet, hoping the keypad combination wasn't written down. It was, posted on a sheet inside the closet door.

I often wonder why I looked for that combination. I certainly did not intend to open the house for Luther. I fully expected Mother to tell him to hit the road after I'd made my case.

I do believe I was testing myself and could only pass the test if I actually *could* open the mansion but *refused* to do it. I certainly would prove nothing by refusing to do something I couldn't do. That's a very sloppy way to explain it but you catch my drift.

I napped fitfully on and off until the fateful moment arrived. It was a moonless night, dark as ink. I stood in the center of the courtyard and listened to the distant churning of the surf.

I waited, hoping against hope they would not appear. However, at the appointed time the big old rusty Cadillac rumbled up to the gate like a prehistoric beast.

I took a deep breath and punched the gate keypad.

When the car pulled to a stop in the courtyard, I ran to Mother, who was driving.

"We need to talk!"

Before she could reply, Luther hopped out and slammed the door. He stared at me over the car roof. "Is the system shut down?"

"No, it's not."

"Why the fuck not?"

I ignored him. "Mother, there never was anything to

inherit. Not from Denton."

"What are you talking about?" Mother asked.

"Did you earn a fucking law degree in one afternoon?" Luther said.

I spoke directly to Mother. "Denton was more or less disinherited. You have to believe me."

Luther bit off a curse. "Shut down the system."

"But you are Denton's daughter and Luther says—" Mother began but her voice was halting and I could tell she was mighty confused at that moment.

"Luther is just plain *wrong*, Mother. You don't need him. He's leading you down the road to ruin."

Luther was on me before I knew it. He grabbed me by the wrist. God, he was strong. "Turn off the fucking security system."

"Do you want me to do that, Mother?"

"You fucking cunt," Luther growled. He bent me back over the fender and suddenly there was a straight razor in his hand. "You shut down that security system now or I will turn your face into a jigsaw puzzle." He forced my legs apart with his thigh.

Luther's eyes went cold, just like they had earlier. At that moment, he didn't care about robbing the house. He was outraged by my refusal and I fully believed he would use the razor just to prove a point.

"Please do what he says, Lila," Mother said. "He means it."

I stared right into Luther's dead eyes. "No."

He touched the cold hard razor to my cheek. I felt the sharp blade crease my skin. I had no idea what I intended to do next.

"Is there a problem, Lila?" A.'s voice cut through the tension of the moment.

Luther relaxed his grip and swiveled to see A. in his tuxedo, standing ten feet away, calming smoking a cigarette.

I'm sure A. saw the razor but there wasn't even a quiver in his voice.

"What the fuck?" Luther muttered. "Get out of here, Gramps. This don't concern you."

"Oh, but I'm afraid it does." His voice was firm and calm.

"Who *is* this guy?" Luther asked.

"Your worst nightmare," I replied. If I hadn't been terrified, I might have actually laughed when I said that.

Luther's face contorted into a mask of frozen fury. After pushing around Mother for so long, he'd forgotten there were people who weren't going to take his shit.

He made this mindless animal noise and pushed me to the ground. Any normal human being would have realized the jig was up and just left. I was definitely thinking a "two persons found dead in botched robbery" sort of scenario was underway.

I grabbed Luther's arm. He pushed me away and turned to face A.

"I suggest you leave the premises immediately," A. said. He nonchalantly flicked his cigarette away.

"Tell him to forget it, Mother!" I shouted but she had her forehead pressed against the steering wheel.

Luther stomped across the ground in long strides, swinging the razor up as though he intended to cut A. in half.

I thought sure I'd seen the end of A., because Luther was twice his size and half his age.

I couldn't watch.

It was over in a flash.

One moment Luther loomed over A. and the next he was on his knees, holding his neck and wheezing for breath as if he had a chicken bone stuck in his throat. A. was crouched above him, right arm extended, a wide space between his thumb and fingers.

He stood. "Lila, come here."

I ran to his side. He put a hand on my hip and slid me

behind his body.

Mother jumped from the car and helped Luther up. Gasping for breath, he slung his arm around her shoulder. She helped him to the passenger side, pushed him into the car and slammed the door shut.

She whirled in my direction, her eyes suddenly full of fire and fury.

"How can you be so selfish?" she hissed. "You *bitch*!"

There was only one thing I could think to say.

"Goodbye, Mother."

She had a great deal of difficulty maneuvering around the fountain, but finally got the car pointed in the right direction and squealed out of the driveway.

30

I ran to the main gate and shoved it shut.

When I turned around, A. was kneeling against the fountain. I hurried to his side.

"Are you hurt? Did he cut you?"

He shook his head. I gently rubbed his shoulders, the only thing I could think to do. After what seemed to be an eternity, he rose and sat on the lip of the fountain.

He flexed his right hand.

"You're hurt."

"It's nothing."

"Nonsense. Come with me."

I shut down the mansion security system and we entered the kitchen. He sat down while I gathered ice from the freezer and put it into a baggie.

"Here," I said. The fleshy part of his hand, between his thumb and forefinger was red and swollen.

I began shaking like a leaf, suddenly overcome by recently transpired events.

"I feel like I'm going to throw up," I said.

"Put your head between your knees and breathe deeply."

I did and gradually the need to barf passed.

"How's the hand?"

"I'll survive."

He applied the ice bag to his hand.

"I suppose I owe you an explanation," I said.

"Your fugitive mother and her boyfriend, no doubt."

"They wanted me help them rob the house."

"Yes."

"My mother—"

He held up his left hand. "Please, spare me."

"I need a drink of water. You?"

He didn't. I fetched a glass of water from the ice water

nozzle on the refrigerator and held it to my brow.

"I thought you were a goner," I said. "Actually, I thought we were *both* goners. Like that movie *In Cold Blood* where the guy kills an entire family because he remembers how much he hated his father?"

He flexed his hand again and set the ice pack aside.

"How did you take him down? Some kind of martial arts, right?"

He ignored the question. "Am I correct in assuming you do not wish to make a police report?"

"No. It would be bad for Mother." I finished the glass of water. "Unless you think I should."

"It's no matter of mine."

He stood and arranged his coat across his shoulders, cape-like.

"Thank you. It was quite brave of you." I clumsily hugged him. He stiffened but I felt his hand touch my back for a brief instant.

"Goodnight, Lila."

After he departed, I sat in the kitchen for a little while longer. A. was the last person I ever thought would come to my assistance. He acted as if I was nothing but a burr beneath his saddle, and there he was, putting himself in harm's way to protect me.

Right there I learned that what people said was meaningless, for actions truly did speak louder than words.

Mother had done me wrong. She had abandoned me and then tried to pull me into Luther's web of crime and deceit. As I walked back to my apartment, I decided that Mother was racing down the road to ruin.

That was a journey she would make without me.

31

The two weeks came to an uneventful end. I didn't see A. once. I didn't bother following him. Somehow, it seemed wrong considering the confrontation with Luther.

I resumed my old routine of morning at the beach and afternoon bike ride. At odd moments, the entire incident with Mother and Luther would flare into my memory. Only in my memory, Luther slashed my face. I shuddered at the thought and chased the image from my mind. I wondered if I should have handled it differently, but all in all, I was at peace with what I'd done.

I assumed Harold would reappear one day and life would go on. As the end of the second week arrived, I thought it would be very nice to have a homecoming party for him.

Chaco was not very enthusiastic.

"Party?"

"Yes, to celebrate Harold's return. We can put balloons on the front gate. I'll get a 'Welcome Home' banner. Maybe you could bake a special cake, something very English."

"What is that, very English cake?"

"You have a hundred recipe books on the shelf, for goshsakes. There must be something English in one of them."

She told me in so many words she couldn't be bothered.

Magda was no help either. When I proposed it to her, she simply nodded in agreement. It was clear I'd have to put together the party by myself.

I hopped on my bike and rode into town. I bought some Mylar balloons and a banner at a party shop and stopped at a bakery.

"A very English cake?" the baker asked. "What is that?"

"Okay, not a cake. Something English."

"Scones?"

"Are they very English?"

"Very."

"Then a dozen scones."

He promised to have them ready the night before. He said it really didn't matter if they were fresh or stale, since they were dry as bone anyway.

Riding a bike while holding balloons isn't the easiest thing in the world, even with them tied to the handlebar, so I just walked the bike home.

I was crossing the courtyard when Magda came running out of the house.

"For you," she said, handing me a FedEx envelope.

I handed the balloons to Magda and tore open the envelope. Inside was a letter typed on thick cream paper with Harold's name and address embossed in classy blue letters.

Dear Lila,

I am unable to return to Sea Spray for the foreseeable future. This has, I'm afraid, placed both of us in a bit of a pickle. As you are undoubtedly aware by now, I took it upon myself to allow you to stay without Mr. Garibaldi's tacit agreement. I did so because of my absolute trust in you and my firm belief that you are better off within the confines of Sea Spray than in Philadelphia.

Alas, due to my protracted absence, your Aunt is now insistent that she receive Mr. Garibaldi's assurance of his guardianship personally. That is, he must call her forthwith and make clear his intentions. If he does not, then you will be forced to depart.

Please prevail upon Mr. Garibaldi to act in an honorable manner.

"Something is wrong?" Magda asked. I felt glum but smiled as she stood there holding the balloons.

"You have children?"

"Yes. Two."

"Take the balloons home then. For the kids."

She smiled. "Is very nice. Thank you."

32

"Mr. Garibaldi, we need to talk."

It was four-thirty in the morning. We were standing outside the cottage.

He took a swig from the silver flask he kept in his tuxedo pocket. He forced a half-smile. "Has your ongoing tale of woe taken yet another ghastly turn?"

"It has."

He motioned me to follow him. Inside, he carefully draped his tuxedo jacket over the back of a chair.

I handed him Harold's letter. He read it and handed it back to me. "We've already been through this."

"Just hear me out. I will not be a bit of trouble. I promise. And I can do things for you."

"What could you possibly do for me?"

"I could make breakfast for you, keep the cottage clean. Run errands. Anything."

"I'm perfectly able to take care of myself." He seemed insulted by the idea he needed anyone to do anything for him.

"All I meant was that you would be doing me a big favor

and I want to repay you. Actually, it's like the third big favor, but who's counting?"

"You do not repay favors. You return them."

"Okay then, I want to return the favor."

He leaned forward, forearms on his knees, and stared at the ground. At that moment, he looked like the loneliest person in the world. Besides me, that is.

"Do you have family? A son or daughter? A brother? A girlfriend?" I asked.

"No."

"See there, we're more alike than you'd like to admit."

He raised his head. "We are?" he said as though I were boring him to death.

"Yes. We are both alone in this life. Fellow travelers, you might say."

He furrowed his brow just a touch. I could tell I'd struck a nerve.

"What could it hurt to have someone to talk to for two months?"

"What makes you think I have no one to talk to?"

"I shouldn't speak for you. What I mean is that it wouldn't hurt for me to have someone to talk to."

"We don't have anything to talk about."

"How do you know? You've never talked to me about anything."

He lit a cigarette. "Let's just say I've already heard enough."

"You think I'm stupid, don't you?"

"I don't think you are stupid."

"It's clear you don't have a very high opinion of me."

"I believe you are intellectually listless, impossibly melodramatic and emotionally overwrought."

He spoke calmly, without any malice in his tone. I felt he was testing me, to see how I would respond.

"First off, I am not intellectually listless. You haven't asked me anything about math. I'm good at math. Straight 'A's."

"I despise math."

"You can't *despise* math. You can't navigate without knowing math."

His facial features sharpened and his body stiffened. "What makes you I think I want to navigate anywhere?"

I cleared my throat but before I could respond, he glanced over at the table where his charts were scattered and then back at me.

He kept on staring until I bit my lower lip. My face grew hot and I knew I was blushing. I decided it was best to fess up.

"I used the security key to sneak in here when you were out at night. Back when I first arrived. I saw the navigation chart for the Dry Tortugas and I figured you were going to sail there." I paused. "I'm sorry. It was the wrong thing to do."

He said nothing.

I stood. "I said I was wrong and I'm sorry and if that's not good enough for you I don't know what! If I am melodramatic it's because my life *is* a melodrama! And I may be a little high strung but I am not overwrought in the least." Then, as I swung open the door, I fired off my final shot. "And being as you *despise* math I hope you get lost and eaten by sharks on the way to the Dry Tortugas!"

I slammed the door on my way out and wondered what I ever found fascinating about Mr. Antonio Garibaldi.

Back in the apartment I sat on the edge of the bed and thought about how I'd let Marla and Harold down. I didn't think A. would turn me in for sneaking into his cottage; somehow, that would be too much trouble. Nevertheless, I truly believed there wasn't a snowball's chance in Hell he would go out of his way for me now.

33

Next morning, I woke to a sharp knock on my door. I tiptoed through the swaths of sunlight and opened the door.

It was A.

"What!"

"I've prepared breakfast. I'd like you to join me."

I was surprised, to say the least. He seemed almost apologetic.

"Give me ten minutes."

I brushed my teeth, rinsed my face and brushed my hair. He was waiting at the bottom of the steps, smoking his cigarette.

"Those things are going to kill you," I noted once more, to no apparent effect.

We walked back to the cottage. He'd made thick waffles for me.

"Now then," he began. "I have thought over last night's conversation. I will honor your request."

I wanted to cry but realized that would be an emotionally overwrought response. "You will?"

"I just said I would, subject to certain understandings."

I folded my hands on my lap and stiffened my back to show he had my full attention. "Go on."

"The first rule is that you are to ask me nothing about my

past or my current comings and goings. That includes not skulking about in my cottage."

"No skulking. Agreed."

"Second, this is a list of eight books you are to read with due diligence in the order listed."

He handed me a piece of paper with a neatly lettered list of books, all unfamiliar to me.

"You will find the books in the library of the main house."

"Yes, sir."

"Third, you will have lunch with me every Saturday at noon. At such time, we shall discuss the book you read that week."

"That's it?" I asked.

"No, that's not it. If you do not follow these rules I will withdraw my sponsorship and dispatch you directly back to Philadelphia."

"I understand. Is that it?"

"No, that's not it. Go back to your apartment. Put on clothes suitable for physical labor, as in jeans, tennis shoes and a T-shirt. Meet me at the front gate in a half hour. And the rule about leaving the estate after dark stands."

I had no idea why he'd changed his mind but I wasn't one

to look a gift horse in the mouth.

I went back to the apartment and dressed as he directed. I met him at the gate and we walked to the end of the driveway, where the red pickup idled with the black driver behind the wheel.

"Otis, this is Lila."

"It's a pleasure to make your acquaintance," he said in a deep, silky voice. "Get on in."

I opened the passenger side door. Otis extended his arm and pulled me into the cab effortlessly.

Antonio slid in next to me.

Classical music played from the dashboard radio. Otis hummed along and tapped his long fingers against the steering wheel. A. stared out of the passenger window. I sat between them and didn't think to say a word.

When we arrived, Otis unlocked the corrugated sliding metal door to the warehouse and slid it open. He motioned me inside with a flourish.

The overhead fluorescent lights flickered on with a soft buzz. In the center of the warehouse sat a row of four fiberglass powerboats on trailers. They were beautiful, sleek and towered over me.

Along the far right wall, engines hung from chains or sat

in a sort of cradle. Red metal cabinets on wheels sat here and there among the engines, drawers pulled open.

"This way," A. said. I followed him past the row of sleek boats. Our footsteps echoed through the oily, still air.

In the far left corner of the warehouse sat a wooden sailboat. With its yellow, tattered sails and faded paint it looked forlorn and forgotten.

"Every day Otis will pick you up at nine. You will work on this boat."

A. handed me a long handled tool with a wide metal blade. "Start scraping. If you have any questions, ask Otis. He'll give you a ride back when you're done."

He strolled away.

I have never considered myself a lazy person but the fact was, I'd never done any real physical labor, other than housework. I made fitful progress until I figured out how to angle the blade just right and use the proper force.

After about an hour my shoulder smarted and my hand was numb. I flexed my hand to get the blood flowing again.

Otis wandered over, a cup of coffee in one hand. He puffed on a pipe. The smoke smelled like vanilla.

He was taller than A. by six inches but moved in the same graceful way. His tight-cropped salt-and-pepper hair flowed unbroken into a salt-and-pepper beard. I figured him to be younger than A. but not by much.

"Got the hang of it?"

"Piece of cake."

"There's a fridge in the office. Cold soda if you need it."

"Thanks. Is this Mr. Garibaldi's boat?"

"It is."

"It's a mess."

"Talking won't make it better."

By two o'clock, I was dreadfully tired and drenched with sweat. Every muscle in my body screamed and I had a nasty blister on my palm.

Every so often the phone would ring and Otis would answer it but otherwise the place was still as a tomb except for the sound of my scraping.

I took a break and walked around the boat. The last owner had painted the words *Big Dick* on the back in gold leaf but it had pretty much faded away. There was a ladder set against the boat. I climbed it.

The deck was made of wooden planks but they were covered with a thick layer of grunge. There was a spoked steering wheel and very large compass inside a brass enclosure. A tarnished bell hung just outside the cabin.

The cabin was a wreck, with old charts and wood tossed this way and that. One of the windows was broken and the other was thick with dust.

I went down three steps and found two platform beds and a dresser built into the wall. There was a curtain in front of each bed for privacy. A door led to a bathroom and tiny shower. A sink filled with dry leaves and a stove with rusty burners sat in one corner.

Otis called down. "Work up a hunger yet?"

I climbed back up to the cabin. "Yes. Should I just keeping working on the bottom of the boat?"

"The bottom of the boat is called the *hull*. The front of the boat is the *bow*. The rear is the *stern, starboard* right, *port* left. Come on, time for lunch."

I followed him into his office. He handed me a baloney sandwich and small bag of potato chips. I was famished.

"Let me see your hands."

I showed him the blisters. He chuckled and fished around in his desk drawer until he pulled out a pair of worn leather work gloves. "Wear these."

"Thanks." I ate my sandwich very quickly. "How do you know Mr. Garibaldi?"

"Funny thing about Mr. G. Just when I think I've seen the

last of him, he comes strolling through the door."

Otis glanced up at the clock. "You've done a good four hours. Why don't I give you a ride home?"

"No, I'll keep working."

"Don't go wearing yourself out on the first day now. Got to get up early tomorrow morning."

"I'm fine. I'm curious though. Could that boat sail on the ocean?"

"Now, some thirty-five's can and some can't. This one can because it has a heavy full keel."

The boat, heavy full keel or not, was a real shambles, not ready for a trip to the Dry Tortugas. Or anywhere, for that matter.

Except for the fact I was obviously out of shape for serious scraping, I didn't mind the work. Memories just flowed through my mind while my arm moved back and forth. Around three, my arm was just dead weight and I had to stop.

I climbed onto the deck and leaned against mast. I listened to tools clang on the other side of the warehouse. I watched small birds flutter high up in the rafters. I felt the slight breeze from the propped open windows cool my sweaty skin while the oily scent that hung in the air filled my nostrils.

At that moment I felt wonderfully, indescribably *alive*,

which, to my way of thinking, is the perfect definition of happiness.

I looked at tarnished brass bell again, and then found Otis, who was using a wrench to tighten a bolt atop one of the engines.

"You have brass polish?"

"Cabinet against the wall. Top shelf. Rags in the bin near the door."

The wrench Otis used was long and had this sort of scale built into the handle.

"What are you doing, exactly?" I asked.

He stopped and looked at me with this bemused expression. "I am properly torquing a cylinder head bolt."

"That's what I thought," I said, smiling.

Otis shook his head and moved the wrench to another head bolt. I found the polish and rag and went back to the boat.

I worked on the bell. An engraved inscription sat beneath the tarnish. It took nearly forty minutes of rubbing to reveal the words: *Commissioned by Harry T. Wales, Designed by Phillip L. Rhodes, 1929.*

"Quittin' time," Otis called as he walked toward the front door.

I glanced at my reflection in the shiny brass for a brief

moment, and then capped the polish.

Otis dropped me off at Sea Spray. He told me he'd see me at nine sharp the next morning.

I dragged myself back to my apartment and took the longest, hottest bath ever. I was too tired to eat, so I just collapsed into bed. I couldn't sleep though. My body was exhausted but my mind was working overtime.

That boat was a shambles, tossed aside and forgotten. Abandoned, so to speak, like someone we all know.

I know what you are thinking. Here goes Lila off on some crazy comparison between her life and some other thing. In my mind, it really made sense, because no one who glanced at that boat would ever think it had any value whatsoever. You had to look under the grunge, tarnish and neglect to see that with some hard work and determination it could one day be something worthwhile.

Like me.

34

Every morning Otis picked me up and I put in a full day at the warehouse. When I broke for lunch he pulled out a big glass jar filled with pickle juice and had me soak my hands for a few minutes. "Toughen up your skin," he explained.

Eventually, my muscles stopped complaining. I spent the

last hour of every day polishing the brass fittings. It made it seem like I was making progress.

I couldn't summon the energy to go to the library in the main house until the Fourth of July weekend. Magda was mopping the kitchen floor when I entered.

"You have a library here, don't you?"

"What is that you mean?" she replied, not looking up.

"Books. A library?"

"Over there," she replied, waving me through the pantry.

The library was on the other side of the music room, behind two pocket doors. Light flooded in through a stained glass dome.

A globe the size of a beach ball sat in the center of the room. The landmasses were raised. I traced my finger along Florida and around the Keys until I found the Dry Tortugas. They felt like grains of sand beneath my fingertip.

The bookshelves were so tall a ladder-on-rails was provided. I considered the number of shelves and the books per shelf and estimated the library held roughly two thousand books.

My first assignment was *We Have Always Lived In The Castle* by Shirley Jackson. After some exploration, I found the thin paperback with a faded cover and yellowed pages.

A wooden circular staircase led to a balcony large enough to hold a leather armchair. A reading light with a tulip-shaped pink shade curved over the back of the chair.

It was oh so quiet inside the library. Surprising how well one can concentrate in the absence of canned laughter of *Brady Bunch* reruns bouncing off the living room walls. I imagined the people who discovered BLACK HOLES sat in a library just like this for days on end.

I've never been much of a reader. I read some of everything I was assigned in school but wasn't one to go to a library and check out books for the hell of it.

I finished the novel in time for my first lunch with A.

He made eggs Benedict. This time he prepared a couple for himself, too.

"Did you see the boat?" I asked.

"You have been quite diligent.

"I keep my promises. Otis said the boat could sail on the ocean." I was hoping A. would reveal his plans but he didn't respond.

"You read the book?"

"Yes."

"And?"

"It was good."

"What do you think it was about?"

"A girl who lived with her uncle and sister. People in the town thought it was her sister who poisoned their parents, but it was the narrator who did it all along."

"That's the plot."

"I know."

He set his fork down. "That's not what the book is about."

"It's not?"

"The plot is simply an artificial ordering of events."

"I don't understand."

"Everything about the book is a conscious choice by the author, Lila. Choosing the first person, for instance, keeps us inside the narrator's point of view. We only know what she tells us."

"Right. So isn't that what the book is about?"

"No."

I sensed his impatience. He lit a cigarette.

"Do you remember the woeful story of your life you told me the first night you talked to me?"

"How could I forget?"

"You breathlessly set forth a series of events, but the point of the story wasn't that the events had occurred. Then it would have simply been a report."

He paused and stared at me.

"I wanted you to understand that I needed your help because my life was a mess?" I said.

"You understand then, the difference?"

"Not entirely."

"Well," he said, flicking the ash from the cigarette, "you will."

On the Fourth of July, I sat on the beach and watched the fireworks explode over the ocean. There was a gently pulsing breeze and I thoroughly enjoyed the show, even though I was alone.

I continued to read as required. By late July, I had finished *The Heart is a Lonely Hunter* by Carson McCullers, *The Optimist's Daughter* by Eudora Welty and *The Collected Stories of Flannery O'Connor*.

"Did you want me to read these because they were written by Southern women?" I asked one day.

"And suppose that is the reason?"

"Is it because women and men look at the world differently?"

"How so?"

"They've written a hundred books about *that*."

"Your opinion on the matter is what I'm interested in."

Funny thing was, until A., no one cared about my opinion. Mother certainly didn't know how she felt about anything, so it probably struck her as odd that I would have any opinions at all. Mother's boyfriends couldn't care less what I really thought because they were obsessed with talking about themselves.

Our first lunch lasted less than an hour. I didn't have the mental stamina to keep up with A., but by the end of July, our talks stretched on for hours. He would ask question after question, gently correcting my grammar or vocabulary, never allowing me to shrug and say 'I don't know.'

This account sounds like our time together was as boring as study hall, but gradually our talks expanded far beyond the books I read. I told him more about my life with Luther and Mother, about my basketball career and Jailbait.com and getting a passport and the day the FBI broke into the apartment.

We toured Sea Spray and he talked for hours about the architecture.

"The colonnade was made popular by the Romans. It was an efficient way to create pockets of shade in public areas."

He was the smartest person I ever met. (Well, okay, that's not saying much.) The historical references he spouted stuck to my brain like lint to a sweater.

I can still see him in the courtyard, pointing out one detail or the other.

"Another word for courtyard is *piazza*. The covered walkway is a *cloister*, *loggia* or *arcade*, depending on the architectural heritage. The interesting treatment of a porch over an entry is a *portico*. The structure at the far end of the pool is a *peristyle*."

It wasn't just that he knew there were words like *oculus*, *plinth* and *voussoir*; he knew where they fit in the history of architecture.

Another time, we walked down to the beach and he asked me how many words there were for the color *blue*. We came up with twenty-two, from *aquamarine* to *sapphire*. (He came up with nineteen.)

He loved words, but then again, he loved architecture, history and literature. I couldn't picture him in a classroom but he was a better teacher than anyone I'd ever encountered.

"What would be the point of a story where the main character attained what she wanted without a struggle?" he asked one Saturday.

"But there must be some stories like that." I argued.

"None that were ever published, I fear. Let's try another tack. What is the central conflict in your life?"

"My life is real. It's not fiction."

"Suppose you wrote a novel about your life."

I really had never thought about the subject, of course, and so I had to ponder that one.

"My central conflict is with my mother," I finally answered.

"How so?"

"She's weak." Saying it made me feel disloyal, recent events notwithstanding.

"But that only becomes a conflict if you are strong and her weakness keeps you from getting what you want. What is it that you want?"

I ran my finger around the rim of the coffee cup. "I just want it all to make sense."

"And her being weak didn't allow that to happen?"

I jumped up and paced back and forth like a wind-up toy, energized by the question. "*Nothing* we ever did made sense. She knew this man, Red Dakota? I think he loved her and wanted to take care of her. We just up and left one day, for no good reason as far as I can tell. Another thing? She wanted to be an actress but never took acting lessons or even tried out for a play." I was surprised at how strong my feelings were. "And during that entire 'let's burgle Sea Spray' scenario she stood there like a coat rack! And Luther held a razor at my face!"

"You believe one should take matters into their own hands?"

"Do *something*, for gosh sakes!" I shouted. I sat down and gathered myself. "I mean, at least I tried to talk you into agreeing to take care of me."

"You might say your mother suffered a sort of paralysis, an inability to take charge of her life, yes?"

"She was like a beach ball, you know? As long as a wind blew, she moved. "

"'Like a beach ball.' And that is?"

"A simile?"

He clapped softly. *"Bravissimo."*

Sometimes I felt he understood me better than I understood myself. Of course, I was always talking about myself.

In the absence of any real information about his life, I constructed my own version. He'd been a screenwriter. He'd known Aunt Rowena when they were both younger. There was no other way to explain why she let him live there. She pined for him all her life (between her marriages, of course.)

The cottage didn't have a phone (though there were phone jacks), a television or radio. He didn't own a car. Magda, who collected the mail every afternoon, couldn't remember a single letter ever being addressed to him.

Why someone so smart and interesting was all alone in the world was beyond me.

Why he dressed in a tuxedo and where he went all night remained a mystery. I did notice another matchbook from the Club Coral on the floor when I cleaned the breakfast table. Neither Magda nor Chaco had ever heard of it.

He'd used martial arts of some sort to bring down Luther, so he must have been a soldier or spy for a little while. (Maybe he knew Earl T. Scomes!)

There was also the matter of his terrible headaches. He often had to stop talking for a bit and gently massage his temples, eyes closed. Other times he grabbed at my arm while we walked and stood motionless for a long while. I just put it off to his drinking, because he consumed far too much for his own good.

As July drew to an end, I had finally reached the point where my life made sense. The boat was being restored and would one day sail again. I read books and A. questioned me. I went for my bike ride and iced caramel macchiato on the weekend, my only days off. For the first time in my life I had purpose and rhythm and routine. My brain was filled with facts

I didn't even know *existed* before Antonio came into my life.

It felt like I'd been at Sea Spray longer than I'd been anywhere. That wasn't technically true, of course, since I'd been in Philadelphia for nearly three years, but never felt like I belonged there. Or anywhere else Mother and I passed through. Sea Spray just *was*, you know, solid and unchanging and I found it all very comforting.

I loved the big pink house, my apartment, and the strolls across the piazza and sunning on the beach. When the oranges ripened the air around the cottage smelled tart and fresh. Those terrible days when I first arrived and felt as though I would never have a life of my own were now a distant memory, as was the point of my being in Palm Beach in the first place.

35

First Friday in August. I was wheeling the bike out of the garage when A. caught up with me. He was dressed in khaki pants, a dark T-shirt and a Panama hat.

"Dude!" I joked.

He stared at me in his disapproving way.

"I meant you look cool. You know? Love the hat."

"Thank goodness you approve," he said in an off-hand way that meant he didn't care whether I liked his hat or not. "Otis and I are departing for a short foray down the coast. I will return Thursday. Until that time, consider yourself on holiday."

On Saturday, I made an appointment at a beauty salon. My hair had grown past my shoulders and was getting to be a real pain, so I had it styled in a chin-length layered side-parted bob I picked out of a stylebook at the salon. It made me look more, well, *sophisticated*.

On Sunday, I resumed my beach-in-the morning, bike-ride-iced-Carmel-Macchiato scenario. I spent a good part of the afternoon in the library reading my next assignment, *Despair* by Vladimir Nabokov, who was neither a woman nor Southern.

By Wednesday morning, I was more or less fit to be tied. I missed working on the boat. I missed knowing A. was around. I finished the book, watched *Sense and Sensibility* again on the VCR and took a long nap. I scrubbed the bathroom until it gleamed. I waited until a quick summer shower ended, then set out on a long, meandering bike ride.

When the sun comes out after a rain, you can catch a rainbow if you look hard enough. (Chasing rainbows is a pretty good metaphor for my life, at that.) You can also find them in puddles on the street and I sort of lost track of where I was going as I sought them out.

I heard a horn behind me and turned to see a bus creeping along. I moved to the side and saw an airbrushed painting of a sunset on the side of the bus. Across the painting was the legend *The Rhythm Kings Featuring Red Dakota.*

How many Red Dakotas could there possibly be?

I followed the bus down a long driveway, past a sign that read "Tropicana Arms Hotel." A few feet away sat a larger, newer sign: "Coming Soon. Tropicana Assisted Living Village. A Bromley Commercial Development."

A lizard skittered across the path as I continued. The 'Tropicana Arms' reminded me of the reclusive relative of 'The Breakers,' a famous Palm Beach hotel.

Unkempt bushes shrouded the building. I wondered how long it would take to scrape the siding down to bare wood, for it was in serious need of a paint job.

A porch with a row of white rocking chairs ran along the entire front of the hotel.

I followed bus exhaust fumes into the parking lot.

The bus parked parallel to the beach, where old wooden beach chairs were stacked next to a half-dozen enormous dumpsters.

The bus doors opened with a pneumatic sigh and the Rhythm Kings filed out, yawning and scratching at their privates, as men are apt to do.

"Red Dakota?" I asked of no one in particular.

"Holy Shit! I'd know that voice anywhere," Red said, emerging from the bus. "If it ain't Smokey Thibideaux herself! Come here darlin'!"

He'd put on a little weight but otherwise hadn't changed a lick. He gave me a big hug. "Let me look at you!" he said, holding me at arm's length. "You have grown into one lovely rose of Texas."

"Don't live in Texas anymore."

"You were there once, and that's good enough." He put his arm around my shoulders. "Boys, this is Smokey Thibideaux. She almost became my stepdaughter. Smokey, meet the boys."

There were twelve of them. They mumbled a greeting, hardly impressed. "We got some catching up to do, don't we?" Red asked. "Come on inside, sweetheart."

The band wandered off lugging their suitcases. "You're staying here?" I asked.

"Staying and playing, honey."

The air inside the bus was ripe with the scent of cigarettes, popcorn and that stale male sweat smell.

"We've got fancy water and all sorts of juice. Don't allow any booze on board. "

"Water will be just fine."

Red handed me a bottle and kicked back on a sofa. I sat

opposite him at a table.

"First things first. How's your momma?"

"She's with another man now."

He looked out of the window with a longing gaze. "She was a lovely woman. You both living down here?"

"I don't live with her anymore. I'm with my Aunt Rowena now. Of the Louisiana Thibideaux?"

He shrugged. "What happened between your mother and you?"

"She got into trouble and I'd rather not go into it. Tell me about the band."

"This year we're gonna play nearly two-hundred and fifty gigs, mostly in the South, though we once got as far north as Cincinnati."

"I bet I know what kind of music you play."

"The only music there is, sweetheart. Big band."

"You sold the car lot?"

"Best decision I ever made. I asked myself, Red, what's the point of barely making ends meet doing something you hate when you can barely make ends meet doing something you love?"

"I can't wait to hear the band. You say you're playing here?"

"Headlining at the one and only Club Coral."

You could've jabbed me with a cattle prod. "Did you say Club Coral?"

"Sure did. Why?"

"Red, I just got to come hear you play."

"Afraid that can't be. See, this is a special sort of night club. Members only."

"You have to help me get inside, Red and that's that."

"Why the blazes are you in such a tizzy about the Club Coral?"

"I've have my reasons."

"It's out of my hands, honey. Members only and you're not a member."

"I can join."

He slapped his knee. "I don't think so."

I wasn't about to let some stupid rule stop me from finally discovering the secret of the Club Coral.

"If I'm in the band they have to let me in, don't they?"

Red leaned forward. "You ain't in the band, honey."

"But I could be, at least for one night. I could sing *Ain't Misbehaving*. Just like the old days, Red. Remember?"

He smiled and stroked his chin. "Indeed I do. Think about them all the time." He winked. "Might be a hoot at that.

Tell you what, we rehearse at five. You show up and show us what you got. It's up to the band. That's all I can promise."

After we talked a bit about the old days, I excused myself and pedaled home fast as I could. I took a long bath. First few times I sang the song my voice cracked, but by the time I toweled off my voice was just fine.

I was certain I'd find A. at the Club Coral and discover what he did at night dressed in his tuxedo. Technically, I realized I was inquiring into his private life but Red was an old friend, so I could pass it all off as a coincidence.

When I returned Red was waiting for me at the back entrance. We walked through the kitchen and down a hallway. We took the back stairs up one floor and through a set of double doors. A sign on the wall read, "Club Coral, Members Only."

The club was dark but I saw recessed lights in the arched, pink ceiling. The floor was hardwood and marked up pretty good from black half-moons I recognized as heel marks.

The Club Coral was a dance hall.

There was a long bar with a matching mirror behind it. And two dozen round wooden tables.

I climbed the steps onto the bandstand.

"Smokey here is going to audition for us. One night only special. *Ain't Misbehaving* good enough?"

I stepped up to the microphone in front of the band. A few soft laughs echoed from behind me.

The microphone screeched.

"Move back a step or two," Red instructed. "Okay, on three."

I had only sung the first verse when Red stopped the band.

"Darlin', you're stiff as a board and sound like you're recitin' the Gettysburg Address! Loosen up. Play to the room. Sell the song."

I understood exactly what he was saying. I was mighty self-conscious at first but eventually relaxed enough to move my hips and shoulders in a sensual way, though not at all trashy.

When I finished the last verse, the band all clapped and hooted.

"I guess you passed the audition. You think you can do that tomorrow night?"

"I think so."

"Okay then. You got a nice dress? Not tight but clingy. Meet us here at nine-thirty sharp."

On the way home I was about as excited as I'd ever been. Except for grade school plays I'd never been on stage, but that did not bother me in the least.

For I would, at long last, uncover the secret of the Club Coral.

36

In the morning, I caught my ride with Otis.

"Have a good trip?"

He waggled his hand. "Had better, had worse. Did something with your hair, girl."

"Yes."

"I like it," he said.

A big pile of junk sat next to the boat. They had obviously gone shopping.

"Went down to the Keys for some salvage. Sails, mast, and whatnot."

"He's really gonna do it, isn't he? Sail to the Dry Tortugas, I mean."

"He's gonna do what he's gonna do."

I noticed right off that someone else had been working on the hull because it had been primed.

"The hull's ready for the cover coat, all gunked and sealed. Today you go top side."

On the deck, Otis handed me a sander with a long electrical cord and showed me how to replace the sandpaper. He gave me a dust mask and dorky safety glasses.

Three days off had given me a new burst of energy. When I took a break, my hands were still vibrating. Except for the strain on my back, it wasn't all that bad.

By noon, I had smoothed the old finish all the way to the main mast. I joined Otis for our usual baloney sandwich and chips.

"Do you own this place?" I asked.

"Lock, stock and barrel. Worked here for a man named Bill Wilson. When he died his relatives in California were only too happy to let me buy the place."

Otis seemed to be in the mood to talk.

"Did Mr. Garibaldi write screenplays?" I asked.

"He was out in Hollywood, yeah. Have no idea what he did."

"Did he ever mention someone named W. Tyler Calderone?"

He shook his head. "Not that I recall."

"How did you meet him?"

Otis glanced at his watch. "You better get back to work." His tone wasn't at all mean but I got the point.

I'd pretty much concluded A. was either W. Tyler Calderone or knew him extremely well.

"Where did he get this boat anyway?" I asked, pulling on

my gloves.

The phone rang and Otis answered it. He turned his back to me and lowered his voice so I went back to work.

Around three o'clock Otis drove me back to Sea Spray. On the way, I had him stop at Neiman-Marcus and I bought a pair of black, seamed pantyhose. I lounged around until around three-thirty, went down to the main house for a snack and started to get ready.

I rehearsed my song in the tub. I wasn't worried about forgetting the lyrics as much as afraid my voice would freeze up if I saw A. in the audience.

I put on make-up and the little black dress I bought for my first meeting with A. and then, to my horror, realized I didn't have any high heels. It was seven o'clock by then and I didn't have time to go back to town. I went down to the main house and punched in the security code.

The mansion was deserted and deathly still. I made my way to the second floor and peeked past every door until I found Aunt Rowena's bedroom. It was simply enormous. Her closet was as large as my bedroom back in Philly.

There were maybe two hundred pairs of shoes. Although you wouldn't reckon it from her general stature, Aunt Rowena had petite feet. Smaller than mine by a half size. I decided to carry the shoes to the Club Coral and only wear them when I sang.

So, all dressed up with somewhere to go, I realized I'd forgotten another minor detail. My only mode of transportation was my trusty bike. I tossed the high heels into my backpack and took off.

The stretch of road between Sea Spray and the Tropicana Arms passed nothing but mansions most of the way, and that created a real problem when it started to rain. Just a few drops fell at first but before I knew it, I was caught in a downpour.

By the time I reached the hotel, a row of limousines filled the driveway. Drivers held umbrellas over the passengers as they hurried toward the shelter of the porch. Getting around them slowed me down even more but finally I pulled open the back door of the club and stumbled inside.

I stood there literally dripping while cooks and waiters bustled about. Steam rose and food sizzled. I caught my reflection in a shiny pan. I had a real Marilyn Manson thing going, what with mascara running down my cheeks and my hair plastered to my forehead.

A black man with a cook's hat on his enormous head shook a ladle at me. "Get your wet ass out of here."

"I'm with the band."

He grabbed another cook and pointed at me. "She's with the band!" Oh, they had a good laugh, they did.

At the top of the stairs was a doorman in a tuxedo. He stepped in front of me, barring my way. The band was warming up just inside the double doors.

"I'm with the band."

The man eyed me suspiciously.

"Just get Red Dakota. He's the band leader."

The man disappeared through the double doors but before they swung shut, I saw the place was pretty well packed.

Red came out dressed in a turquoise dinner jacket with a white carnation in his lapel.

"Look like something the cat drug in, darling. Can't go on like that."

Red handed me his room key.

"Go up to room two hundred and pretty up. Come on, time's a wasting."

The doorman spoke for the first time. He had a French accent. "Take the stairs." He pointed to a door.

Inside Red's bathroom, I scrubbed the makeup off. I hadn't brought any with me but nothing I could do about that. I used his hair drier on my hair and dress. By the time I was done I'd calmed down considerably. I carried the shoes and slipped them on before I walked through the double doors.

The amazing thing about the Club Coral was that everyone inside the club had to be at least seventy years old. We're talking serious silver hairdos. Women outnumbered the men by at least two-to-one, so it was more or less like being in a room with fifty replicas of my aunt. Stepford Rowenas. The Rhythm Kings were playing and ballroom dancing was in full swing.

Then I saw him.

A. was right smack in the middle of the dance floor, looking very handsome in his tux. I was transfixed by the graceful, self-assured way he swirled his partner across the floor.

The song ended. The woman A. danced with pressed something into his hand. I took it for her phone number written on a piece of paper. I concluded that A. probably spent every night in bed with a different woman and that explained why he was out until dawn.

I made my way through the crowd to the bandstand.

"You ready, honey?" Red asked.

"Yes."

"Knock 'em dead."

He stepped to the microphone.

"Ladies and gentlemen, we have a treat for you tonight.

Making her debut tonight with the Rhythm Kings is Ms. Lila Thibideaux, who will favor us with her unique song stylings."

The whole world seemed to stop. I felt like I was underwater. The only sound I heard was the click of my high heels as I wobbled to the microphone.

Every eye in the place was locked on me. I mean to tell you, the butterflies in my stomach were seriously aflutter, in addition to which my feet felt like someone had clamped them into a vise. I swallowed a few times to make sure my throat wasn't bone dry.

The band started. A. moved to the back of the crowd. I couldn't tell whether he was angry or surprised, but it didn't matter right then anyway.

After the first bar, I was fine. The only problem was, no one danced. They all stared at me, swaying slowly to the beat.

To this day, I don't remember actually singing the song, but I must have because when I finished the folks applauded and whistled. Someone shouted "Encore!"

"Sounds like you folks want to hear another. How 'bout it, Smokey?" Red winked.

Well, no point in denying the public.

"Keeping Out of Mischief," I whispered.

A. had moved closer to the bandstand and stood with his

arms crossed over his chest. From my vantage point, I could tell he was not happy with my presence.

When I finished, there was another round of applause. It was a wonderful feeling to have a roomful of strangers signal their approval and my face went hot from embarrassment.

"Now, we've got to send this little darling home. It's past her bedtime."

Red gave my hand a squeeze. "Nice job, sweetheart," he whispered. As I walked toward the bandstand steps, I passed Antonio walking in the direction of Red. He ignored me.

"And now," I heard Red announce, "we have a request for a waltz."

The band struck up and A. waited at the bottom of the bandstand steps. He extended his hand. I realized he wanted me to dance with him.

"I can't dance. Not a waltz."

He took my hand.

"Wait." I took off my high heels and he swept me onto the floor.

It was marvelous! Like gliding on air. His hands guided me this way and that. I had no idea what I was doing but I figure it was my mother's dancing past that kept me from making a fool of myself.

"What are you doing here?" he asked.

"I know Red from my Texas days. I thought it would be fun to sing."

"I doubt this is a coincidence."

"Why, Mr. Garibaldi, how would I possibly know you danced here?" I teased him in my best Scarlett O'Hara imitation.

He gave me a severe look and I smiled in spite of myself.

"I just wanted you to know what you did at night."

"It's none of your business what I do at night, Lila. And you are not supposed to off the estate after dark."

"Oops."

The song ended. He released me. "You've had your fun. Go home." He walked away and I headed for the door.

A woman with a puffy face and pink dress stopped me. "Such a unique voice. A young Peggy Lee! I could listen to you all night!"

"Thank you."

"And you danced with Antonio! Isn't he positively divine?" The band started up again. "Oh, the tango! I must dance the tango with Antonio!"

She bustled off in his direction but another woman beat her to the punch. There were fewer people on the dance floor now, being as the tango is not the sort of dance you can make up as you go along. A. was the center of attention. The tango is one sensual dance and it was amazing how smooth A. moved.

"You are not related to Rowena Thibideaux, by any chance?" a woman wearing a mess of a purple dress asked as she eyed me coldly.

"She's my aunt. I'm staying at Sea Spray for the summer."

"Indeed."

The puffy-faced woman found me. "It's impossible to get on his dance card, you know."

"I can imagine."

"He is the last true gentleman, you know, so very gallant."

I almost laughed because the puffy-faced woman had to be in her seventies and she was acting like someone, well, my age. "He never takes a tip," she whispered to me.

"You tip him to dance?"

"Oh, we *pay* him to dance, of course. Some of the others, well, if you don't tip them they give you that look. Not Antonio."

The song ended and she headed off in his direction again. He glanced my way and I felt a wave of sadness wash over me.

"*Vous ete merveilleux chantuese,*" the doorman said.

"*Merci,*" I replied, surprised I remembered my French. "You see that man on the dance floor? The one with the silver hair?"

"Mr. Garibaldi?"

"Yes. Why do people pay him to dance?"

"It is his job, mademoiselle."

"His *job*?"

The man swept his hand in the direction of the crowd. "The women here, they have all outlived their husbands. They are all very rich but very lonely. They come here to dance, perhaps to forget, perhaps to recapture their youth. And so they pay Mr. Garibaldi, and the others. But he is the most popular."

"I can see why."

"They all say the same thing about him."

"What's that?"

"They say he is . . . a dreamboat."

I walked through the double doors out into the parking lot. The rain had stopped. The surf boiled up onto the beach.

I put on my tennis shoes, retrieved my bike and walked home. I was truly exhausted, but not in the same way as a day on the boat tired me.

I had been nervous about singing, amazed the audience was so appreciative, fearful of upsetting A., exhilarated by dancing with him and saddened by his disapproval. The entire freaking gamut of emotions, as they say.

It was all too much for a girl to bear!

I had solved the mystery of Club Coral. But I sensed I had hurt A. I suppose it was hard him to swallow that he now had to dance with rich old lonely women for a living. Maybe he thought I would think badly of him.

Suddenly, I wanted to go back to the Club Coral, pull A. off the dance floor, and bring him back to the cottage where we could drink espresso and talk about novels and architecture and all the things that made him so very special.

I decided to leave well enough alone and went to bed.

37

Otis didn't pick me up the next morning.

I waited until nine, went back for my bike and rode to the warehouse. Otis' truck wasn't there and the outer gate was locked.

Back at the estate, I checked the cottage. A. didn't answer the door.

I walked back into the main house and asked Chaco if she had seen Mr. Garibaldi or if he'd left a message, but she just shrugged.

Since I had time on my hands, I headed back to the Tropicana Arms to thank Red for letting me sing.

I went up on the elevator and knocked on his door.

"Yeah?" he called.

"It's Smokey."

"Hold on."

He opened the door in his bathrobe as he scrubbed his hair with his free hand. "What time is it?"

"Around one."

"Something wrong?"

"I just wanted to thank you. For last night."

"Glad to do it. You were a hit. If you were a mite older I might just take you on the road." He opened the door. "I was going to have some lunch. Care to join me?"

"No, thank you."

"Tell me, what was the big deal about you having to sing last night?"

"It doesn't matter now."

"You missed all the excitement. Seems one of the dancers sort of outdid himself."

"Really?"

"Handsome older man." He brightened. "Come to think of it, the guy you danced the waltz with. He was taken away in an ambulance."

My body went numb.

"Is he—?"

"He was alive when they took him away, from what they say."

I took a deep breath. "I got to run." I kissed him on the cheek. "Thanks for everything."

At the front desk, I inquired as to the hospitals in the area. There were two. They didn't know where A. had been taken. They gave me directions to the closest one.

I was beside myself, of course. Who knew how many times he'd fainted when I wasn't around?

By the time I reached the first hospital, I was drenched in sweat. My mouth was dry, my heart pounding. I couldn't bear the thought that A. was dead.

I went up to the information desk.

"I'm looking for a patient. He came in last night. His name is Antonio Garibaldi."

The woman checked the computer. "I'm sorry. We don't have a patient by that name."

"You mean he was released?"

"He was never admitted."

The woman gave me directions to the next hospital. It was located on the other end of the county, too far to ride my bike.

"Do you have the phone number?" I asked, realizing I

probably should have called both hospitals in the first place.

I slipped into the lobby phone booth and called the second hospital.

"Do you have a patient named Antonio Garibaldi?"

"Are you family?"

"His grand-daughter. Please tell me."

A long pause. "He was released about a half hour ago."

"So he's okay?"

"He was released."

I hung up and sat in the booth for a moment, gathering myself. He was fine. They wouldn't have released him otherwise, I told myself.

When I returned to the estate, I went directly to the cottage. I knocked but A. didn't answer.

"Antonio, it's me. Please let me in."

I felt he had to be inside. Where else could he be? I had no idea where Otis lived, or even his last name. I went back to the apartment and stared up at the ceiling fan until I fell asleep.

I woke around five. As I rode to Starbucks, I felt as though the world had stopped making sense and that bothered me terribly.

I rode back to the warehouse but Otis was nowhere to be found, so I meandered back to my apartment and channel-changed until I finally fell asleep.

38

The next morning I waited at the top of the drive but Otis didn't show. I had been thrown off my regular schedule and felt at loose ends. I thought about taking a swim but didn't even have the energy to go back to the apartment and change into my bathing suit.

I walked down the driveway and opened the main gate. I heard a truck door slam. I looked back to see Otis' truck pull away and A. walk toward me.

"Where have you been?" I snapped.

He stopped and studied me. He didn't look any worse for wear, although he was still in his tuxedo.

"I believe you have our roles reversed. I'm supposed to worry about you." He strolled away.

"You were in the hospital, for chrissakes!"

He stopped, clearly surprised. "How do you know that?"

"Never mind how I know! Why didn't you have Otis tell me what's going on?"

"Why do you need to know what is going on?"

"Did it ever occur to you that I might actually care what happens to you?"

"I'm going to go back to my cottage, now," he said,

clearly fighting to maintain his patience. He walked away. I walked along side him.

"Wait a minute. You didn't answer my question."

"Precisely which question, of the many you have posed, do you want me to answer?"

"Did it ever occur to you that I might care about what happens to you?"

He pulled up short. "Listen carefully. I do not want you to care about me."

He walked away again.

I didn't follow but shouted out, "Yeah, well that's too bad because I do care about you! And as we both know, when I get an idea into my head it's not *ever* gonna leave! So you just keep walking but whether you like it or not I am attached to you tighter than a tick on a hound, Mr. Antonio Garibaldi!"

He stopped but didn't turn around. After a long moment, he started walking again. I didn't say anything else. I didn't have to.

I changed into my work clothes and rode down to the warehouse, pedaling fast and hard to release my anger. I skidded to a stop next to Otis' truck, hopped off the bike and bent at my waist, catching my breath.

Otis was inside at his desk, puffing on his pipe as he

shuffled through a bunch of invoices. He made entries in an old-fashioned green ledger.

I stood there, tapping my toe.

"You can do that on a computer, you know."

"Mmm-hmmm," he said but didn't look up.

"You gonna tell me what's going on?"

"Going on?"

"Duh! You didn't pick up me for two days. I thought we had a deal."

"Your deal was with Mr. G."

I leaned against the doorjamb. "That's right, I did. And I'm going to work now."

I walked over to the boat, pulled on my dust mask and started power sanding. After ten minutes, the power died.

Otis climbed onto the deck. He held the plug end of the power cord.

"No point in doing this now," he said. "Go home."

"What are you talking about? There's half a deck to sand."

Otis took his pipe from his mouth and stared into the bowl. "Talk to Mr. G."

"He won't talk to me." I stood, brushing the sawdust from my pants. "Come on, Otis, give a girl a break. What the hell is going on?"

"It's none of my affair."

"Hey, we eat baloney sandwiches together. That counts for something."

He motioned for me to sit on the gunwale. "Me and Mr. G. go back a long ways. We've been in and out of all sorts of scrapes. But I can't tell you what he won't."

"I get it. Some kind of Butch Cassidy and the Sundance Kid male bonding horseshit."

Otis glared at me but I pressed on.

"I care a great deal about him, whether he wants to admit it or not, so I want to know what's going on."

"He wouldn't take kindly to me telling secrets."

"Okay, I'll ask the questions. You just answer yes or no." That's how the reporters got information in movies.

"Go ahead," he said after a pause.

"He was going to restore this boat and sail to the Dry Tortugas."

"Yes."

"And something happened the other night that made him change his mind."

"Yes."

"It has something to do with why he went to the

hospital."

"Yes."

"And he told you not to tell me what it was."

"Yes."

I didn't have any other questions.

"I'll just keep working, if you don't mind. I don't have anything else to do."

"Lila, there's only so much work you can do. And then we need money to get the motor rebuilt."

"Antonio doesn't have any more money, is that it?"

He clamped the pipe between his teeth. "That's all I'm gonna say. If he wants to tell you more, that's up to him."

Being as I was all dusty anyway, I decided to work the rest of the day.

The deck was made of planks and the sawdust was reddish. It was clearly made of a different wood than the hull, which was very light brown.

I finished around four. Otis waited by the door.

"What is the deck made of?"

"Teak. Holds up well in the salty air." He pulled the big door shut and padlocked it.

"What do you cover it with?"

"You mean what finish do we use?"

"Yes."

"We were planning on using a teak finish. Listen, you want to throw your bike in the back? I'll give you a lift home?"

"No. I'm fine."

When I returned to the estate, I went directly to the cottage and rapped on the door. A. opened it a crack.

"Just for the record, I kept my side of our agreement."

39

When I arrived at the cottage of Saturday, A. hadn't cooked lunch. I didn't say anything about that. I just sat down across from him.

"*Despair*, by Vladimir Nabokov, is a first-person narrative about a man who has sex with three different women on the same day."

That wasn't what the novel was about, but I was trying to get a reaction from him. I did. He eyed me calmly for a long moment.

"Rather than acting like a petulant child, just say what's really on your mind." He spoke in that calm, detached tone that sometimes infuriated me.

"The world doesn't make sense anymore and you know how that causes a real conflict for me."

He lit a cigarette, took a deep drag, and let the smoke curl out of his nostrils. "Lila, the world doesn't make sense to anyone."

"That's not true. Last week everything made sense. We were restoring the boat, I was reading the books, and we were having our Saturday talks. Suddenly we're not working on the boat and I know something is going on because no one will tell me what's going on."

"Nothing is, as you put it, *going on.*'"

I leaned forward. "You're a liar, Antonio Garibaldi. And you know me well enough to know I will get to the bottom of this, come hell or high water." I had never spoken to him like this and I thought he would fire back with some obscure reference.

Instead, he slumped in his chair, as if he knew he didn't have the energy to put me off any longer.

I reached out and touched his knee, softening my tone. "I care for you. Why is that so hard for you to understand?"

"I understand!" he barked. It was the first time he'd ever raised his voice.

"What's so terrible about having someone care about you?"

He glanced at his watch but he was just stalling.

"Tell me, Antonio. Just tell me the truth."

He stubbed out his cigarette. "Very well then. Since you insist on the brutal truth, here it is. I'm dying." He said it without emotion, almost as if he was telling me where he was born.

My blood ran cold. Literally. I began to shiver.

"Does the world make sense to you now?" he asked gently.

I grabbed his silver cigarette case and flung it across the room. "Lung cancer, isn't it? Goddamn cigarettes!"

He calmly went over, retrieved the case and returned to his seat. "A tumor has wrapped itself about my brain like an octopus."

"That's better!" I said. "You can get it operated on! They have lasers that can cut out anything!"

"There's nothing that can be done."

"Of course there is!" I persisted.

He laughed softly. "I can undergo an operation with almost no chance of success, subject my body to chemotherapy and radiation and slowly waste away. I suppose that is something."

My arms hung limply at my side. My mind scrabbled to find something, anything to say, but it was as though I'd been struck dumb.

We sat in silence for a long time. Finally, he stood and gathered the plates.

"I'll do it," I said, jumping to my feet.

I carried the plates into the kitchen and filled the basin with hot soapy water. I plunged my hands in and held them there until I couldn't stand it anymore. The pain brought me back to my senses.

I dried my hands. "Does it hurt?"

"Hurt?" He snickered. "No, it doesn't hurt. A little pressure now and then."

"That's why you faint, isn't it?" I asked as I entered the living room.

He nodded.

I sat on the sofa and said nothing for a long time. I had no idea what *to* say, to be honest. Finally, just to break the tension, I said, "You are a wonderful dancer."

"And you are a wonderful singer."

"Honest?"

"Indeed."

"Did I do wrong? I mean, did I embarrass you?"

"You didn't do anything wrong, other than to violate the agreement we had made concerning your whereabouts during the night."

"Sorry."

"Forgiven." He studied me for a moment. "Your hair."

"Do you like it?"

"I do. "

More silence descended. I felt like I was hanging on a root as I dangled over a cliff, fighting desperately to regain my footing, fighting for every inch, before I dropped into the abyss.

"I'm going to keep working on the boat," I said firmly.

"Don't waste your time."

"I want to keep reading the books, too. And have our Saturday lunches. I want everything to stay the same. Everything."

His eyes narrowed and he kneaded his forehead.

"Here, lie down," I said, helping him over to the sofa. "And I'm going to keep an eye on you whether you want me to or not. Understand?"

"I understand," he said with a weary sigh.

40

A dark cloud hung over every moment of my life from that day forward. I spent hours on the Internet, looking up brain tumors, trying to learn as much as I could, but what it boiled down to was if the tumor was inoperable, so be it. There was no magic wand available to make A. better.

The work on the boat continued. Otis and I sealed the deck and painted the hull. This took nearly a week, given all the preparations required between coats.

I finished polishing all the brass. Otis informed me the proper nautical term for the brass fittings was *brightwork*.

The boat looked a thousand times better than when I started, although the cabin was in need of complete refitting.

Otis pitched right in. It didn't seem to matter to him that A. would probably never sail it. He said the boat could be sold and he'd pay me a share for the work I'd done out of the profits.

One day Otis motioned me to the rear of the boat and pointed to the spot where *Big Dick* once been painted.

"Every boat needs a name. And since you've been putting in the sweat, choose one."

Well, there was no doubt in my mind at all.

"Dreamboat."

He said he knew a man who owed him a favor. When I reported for work, a few days later, the name I chose was there in fancy gold letters. It looked great.

An enormous feeling of pride welled up inside of me. I was happy I hadn't quit and left the job half-done. I wasn't going to quit on A. either.

I visited him every day. When he wasn't sleeping, he was

drinking and smoking cigarettes. He never mentioned the boat and I didn't bring it up.

He no longer went to the Club Coral. He said he didn't want to make a spectacle of himself by falling on the floor.

He seemed to welcome my visits and I enjoyed making them. He taught me to make espresso in his old copper lever machine.

"If you are the smallest amount off when pulling your shot, the results in the cup will show it," he explained. I learned about crema, the foam that floats on the top of a perfect espresso, types of coffees and the proper grinds. Eventually, I learned to tolerate espresso with a single sugar cube.

A. was usually under the influence, but he wasn't a mean or falling-down drunk. Instead, he became expansive and revealed more and more about his past.

The table outside the cottage was where he was most relaxed and talkative. Maybe it was the smell of oranges and sound of the surf, or perhaps it was just being in the fresh air.

I drank my espresso and he his liquor.

He told me he spent time as a safari guide in Kenya. He'd been a commercial fisherman, a stevedore and spent time in Istanbul and Morocco, "keeping an eye on things" (what those things consisted of, he didn't specify). He'd also lived in Italy for many years.

I surprised him by looking up information on his namesake, Giuseppe Garibaldi, a revolutionary leader who had united Italy. That set him off on a long oration about the beauty of Tuscany. A week later, he had a tray set with Tuscan pork specialties he'd had Chaco special order: *arista, coppa nalla testa, proscuitto and capicolla.* He didn't eat any but explained in intricate detail the differences between them.

I felt as though he was afraid he would die with all his knowledge stuck in his head and he wanted to share as much as humanly possible. I was, of course, more than willing to accept the gift.

41

Since the walls around his past had come down, one day I sort-of-accidentally found the screenplays.

"What are these?" I asked.

"Screenplays."

"Who is W. Tyler Calderone?"

"'Tis I."

"Does this mean you lived in Hollywood?"

"For several years I toiled as a poorly paid, much abused contract studio writer."

I didn't let on that I was familiar with the Townsend

scandal story, though I itched to hear his version of the events. I let a few days pass and printed off the story of the scandal.

"You know, I came across this story on the Internet. It's about one of your scripts, I think."

He wanted to see the story, so I gave it to him. He read it and set it aside.

"It's a sad story," I said after a while.

"It is," he said. "A very sad story."

"Do you know why Townsend killed Katherine?"

He made a steeple with his fingers and tapped them together as though not quite certain he wanted to answer the question. Finally, however, he did. "He killed Katherine because of me."

He ran his hands through his hair and lit a cigarette. I thought he was going to continue, but he didn't.

"You can't just drop a bombshell like that and not tell me more," I pleaded.

He shrugged. "I was under contract with his studio. Townsend came up with ideas and wrote them on scraps of paper. They were all the same story really."

"Two men in love with the same woman?"

"Yes. Katherine—." He paused and went over to a travel trunk. He rummaged about until he found a picture. He stared at it as he walked back to the sofa, and then handed it to me.

It was of him and Katherine standing on a beach. She was absolutely beautiful. She wore a flowing white off-shoulder dress. He was in a pair of chinos and a short sleeve white shirt, open at the collar. They were young and it was clear they were happy just be on that beach with one another.

"Were you in love with her?"

He rubbed his temples. "She was, alas, the only woman I ever loved."

It was an incredible revelation, considering he once forbid me to ask anything about his past.

I leaned forward with rapt anticipation. "Tell me more."

He fiddled with his hands. "We were young and foolish. She wasn't married to Townsend, of course, but just the same." His voice trailed off.

For once, I kept my mouth shut. After a long moment, he spoke again.

"We were going to run off. She thought it was only right to tell Townsend." He cleared his throat. "I went on ahead. She was to meet me in Miami Beach. From there we were going to—." His voice faded once more. "What's to tell? She told him, he shot her and then himself."

"That's terrible." Was it possible he loved her so much

he'd spent his entire life in mourning? How incomparably romantic!

"How did you hear?"

"On the radio. For a week you couldn't pick up a newspaper without reading about it."

He leaned back and closed his eyes. "These things happen and you wonder if you could have done things differently."

I was reminded of how I felt the night I made the break with Mother. You do what you think is best and move on.

Another long stretch of time passed.

"Where were you going?"

He sat up. "What's that?"

"You said you and Katherine were going somewhere."

He gave a short laugh, in that way he snorted through his nose. "We were going to sail into the sunset."

I already knew the answer to my next question but asked it anyway.

"To the Dry Tortugas?"

He looked at me and I found the answer in his eyes.

Yes, yes, *yes*! What a magically tragic story! After Denton left Mother and she stumbled through a lifetime of worthless relationships, I can't tell you what sitting across from man who knew the meaning of true love meant to me.

I thought: here I am, with a seafaring man in my past (hung from a yardarm, but just the same) and a man in my present who wants to sail to the Dry Tortugas because that's where he and his true love were going before she was murdered.

However, he cannot go because he has an inoperable brain tumor.

Connect the dots. A. was the most important person in my life. He'd saved my face from being sliced into ribbons, if not my very life. He'd let me stay at Sea Spray even though he had no cause to put himself out. He'd taught me a million things. We danced a waltz together. Let's just say I owed him. Big time.

In return, I decided to help him sail to the Dry Tortugas, come hell or high water.

42

"Sail to the Dry Tortugas? First off, the boat isn't finished. Second, a man in his condition cannot be out on the ocean alone. It's dangerous out there." Otis shook his head as he eyed me.

"I'm going with him."

"What do you know about sailing?"

"Nothing. But I will learn."

"Go away with that talk now." He packed his pipe. "Besides, he's got no money to finish the boat."

"I have money."

"You've got at least a grand?"

"I'll get it."

"What you thinking about doing, girl?"

"Never mind that right now. If I got the money, we could make the trip, couldn't we?"

He lit the pipe and puffed. "Get the engine rebuilt. A few odds and ends. Yeah, you could make the trip. What does A. say about this?"

"He doesn't know."

Otis walked away, muttering under his breath.

I had no idea what Luther's diamond necklace was worth. But I would gladly trade it for the money to finish the boat.

Of course, none of this many any sense if A. wasn't interested in my proposition.

I broached the subject at our Saturday breakfast, just after we finished discussing *A Moveable Feast*.

"I think you should make that trip to the Dry Tortugas."

"Impossible. The boat isn't finished."

"Beside that."

"I'm dying."

"Beside that."

He had no answer.

"The boat will be finished. I'll make sure it is."

"Who's the one with the brain tumor here?"

"I am definitely not being melodramatic, but I will not let you just sit here and wait to die."

"Lila, you're letting your enthusiasm get the better of your common sense."

"I'm really good at math and I'm a quick study. I can learn to read a navigation chart. I've been working all these weeks and I'm as fit as I've ever been."

"I can see you're smitten with the romantic implications of this proposed endeavor, but I suggest you forget about it and throw you energy into writing a lachrymose romance novel instead."

I stood up and leaned on the back of the kitchen chair.

"I'll forget about it when you tell me honestly that you don't want to sail to the Dry Tortugas before you die."

He didn't respond one way or the other, which was all the encouragement I needed.

43

I had no idea what my pendant was worth.

I called two jewelry stores and asked them if they would buy a diamond pendant from me. They acted as if I asked for a loan. Retail trade only. One told me to find a pawnshop.

I was just short of eighteen but I knew that if a young, pretty girl needs something done, well, she just has to find the right man.

If you catch my drift.

That afternoon I made up my face and caught the trolley to the shops. I bought a new little black dress, a pair of high heels, black seamed stockings and a floppy wide-brimmed hat. I put them on in the store but asked for the boxes to go.

I stopped at two jewelry stores but when women waited on me, I made small talk and moved on.

At the third store, a salesman approached, rubbing his hands together. Short and rotund, he was dressed in a double-breasted suit. His shoes were so shiny they looked like plastic. He wore a small gold name badge that read 'Anton.' His hair was neatly combed and he smelled of way too much cologne. I figured him to be somewhere in his mid-fifties, give or take. He had very greedy eyes.

"Good afternoon. Might I be of assistance?"

"Perhaps you can. I'm Lila Thibideaux?" I struggled with my packages. He quickly took them and set them on the counter.

"Thibideaux? Rowena Thibideaux is one of our most treasured customers."

"She's my aunt. I'm staying at Sea Spray for the summer."

He stepped back, spreading his arms expansively. "Diamonds."

"Excuse me?"

"I look at you and I see diamonds. Perhaps a tasteful necklace?"

I took his arm in mine, making certain his elbow was tucked against my breasts and led him toward a display case. "Anton, I have a slight problem."

"A woman so young, so beautiful! What problem could you possibly have?"

I watched those greedy eyes play over my body. He might well have already seen my perfect little ass on Luther's website.

"I have something I'd like you to look at."

"But of course."

He stroked my upper arm before he walked behind the display case and removed a black velvet square. "It would be my distinct pleasure."

I set the pendant on the velvet. He clapped his hands together. "Lovely. Exceptional." His fingers were fat as sausages. He wore a wedding ring.

"What do you think this is worth?"

"A moment, please," he said, taking the pendant and

disappearing behind a door at the rear of the store.

I noticed a woman for the first time standing behind a display case at the opposite side of the store. She glanced up at me and smiled. I wandered over.

"Hello."

"Good afternoon," she replied. "My husband is helping you?" She was very thin, with well-tanned Botox skin.

"Yes, he is. I'm Lila Thibideaux. Rowena Thibideaux's niece?"

"Yes! I am Giselle Clemenceau. Rowena mentioned you would be staying at Sea Spray this summer."

"I'm going to Paris next month," I replied.

She clapped her hands together. "The city of lovers! Before you depart, you must call me for lunch. I will tell you of the best places to go, places tourists never see."

She took out her card and wrote her down her phone number. "I will give you my private number."

"Thank you very much."

I went back to the counter and sat on a stool, making certain my dress rode up my thigh.

Anton returned, smiling broadly, his eyes fixed on the skin of my thigh. "Beautiful," he said.

"Excuse me?"

"The diamond. One-point five carats. Flawless."

"That's good?"

"Oh, exceptional. Whoever bought it for you must have loved you very much."

"It's a long story." I leaned over the display case. "Mother was so upset, my receiving a gift from an older man."

"I understand," he said. "Completely."

"And what do you think it is worth?

"If we had this in the store, nine thousand. Remounted of course. The setting does not match the quality of the stone."

I nearly swooned. Luther bought it hot, if not outright stole it.

"I do hope it is insured."

I ignored the question. "I don't suppose it's possible to sell it."

He grinned. "Sell it? Well, I suppose you could put it on eBay."

I leaned forward. "Let's just say I would do almost anything if I could dispose of this quickly," I whispered.

I let the idea hang in the air. He cleared his throat. "Perhaps something could be arranged."

"That would be wonderful."

He glanced at his watch and lowered his voice to a

whisper. "I close the store at five. We could meet at Chez Maison at six?"

I smiled. "If you're sure I'm not putting you out."

"Not at all." He opened a drawer and placed the necklace in a black velvet case.

"Shouldn't we discuss the arrangements now?"

His eyebrows knitted. "Arrangements?"

"Anton, I'd love to go to the Chez Maison with you tonight and perhaps somewhere else after that, but I think it's best not to mix business with pleasure."

He cleared his throat. "Yes, well." He drummed his fat fingers against the display case. "I couldn't sell the diamond in the store, of course. Its provenance is uncertain. However, I do have buyers who might be interested in such a brokered purchase. The markup on my end would not be as great as in a traditional retail transaction, so I could offer you, say, one thousand dollars?"

"A thousand?" I ran my tongue across my lower lips. "Could we say fifteen hundred?" I nervously glanced toward the rear of the store, but Giselle had disappeared into the back room. I smoothed his necktie. "I assure you it will be money well spent."

He blushed and looked away. "Very well then. I will have

a cashier's check for you tonight."

The way I figured it, he was going to make a pretty penny on his purchase. He probably wouldn't even bother to claim it on his income tax.

When I walked out of the store, I knew exactly what I had more or less promised. How was I going to get the money without Anton feeling appropriately appreciated? I just decided to take things one step at a time and think on my feet as best I could.

There was a bookstore across the street. I went inside and took a seat near the window, idly leafing through magazines. Around five, Anton exited with Giselle. He spent a good deal of time explaining something to her, glancing at his watch. He kissed her on the cheek. She drove off in a Lexus. He went back into the store.

Chez Maison was a small brick building with a gold nameplate. It only held around fifteen tables. The maitre d' smiled and bowed when I entered.

"A table for one, *Mademoiselle*?"

"Two."

Anton arrived ten minutes later. He had recharged his cologne.

"*Mon Cherie*," he said, kissing my hand.

We were shown to a table in the rear. A waiter appeared immediately and filled our water glasses. "May I show you a wine list?"

Anton wanted one. It was leather bound. He ordered and handed the list back. When the waiter left, Anton patted his chest over his heart. "I have the cashier's check."

"And I have the diamond," I said playfully.

The waiter made a big deal of opening the bottle and Anton made a bigger deal of sniffing the cork. I took a sip but was never a fan of alcohol.

Anton took a generous swig and swallowed hard. His knee pressed against mine and I let my legs part a bit.

"I want you to know I do not normally do this."

"Eat here?"

He stared at me blankly, and then smiled. "You jest."

He poured himself more wine and then stared down into the glass. "I am very much in love with my wife, but our marriage has, shall we say, grown cold."

I reached out and patted his hand. "You don't need to explain."

He relaxed considerably. "I have a wonderful surprise. A good friend of mine has agreed to loan us his yacht for this evening."

"That sounds very romantic. What is your friend's name?"

"Phillipe." His voice rose upward as he said the name.

"Will you excuse me?" I said. "I need to visit the little girl's room."

He nodded and sipped more wine.

Inside the bathroom, I pressed my face against the cool tile. I had no doubt Anton would complete the transaction after we did whatever on the yacht. I faced the prospect of, at the very least, being groped by sausage fingers.

I stared at my face in the mirror. I'd gone this far and the money was within my grasp. It was one of those ethical decisions, like pushing a button that would kill Hitler and save the world from war. Hardly as world-shaking as that, but you catch my drift.

There was no point in forestalling the inevitable. When I opened my purse to find my lip-gloss, I saw the business card Giselle had given me and right there an idea popped into my head.

I joined Anton at the table and he ordered some veal dish for each of us. He made small talk and I kept pouring him wine. There didn't seem to be any limit to how much he could drink but finally, halfway through dinner, his bladder was full to bursting.

When he excused himself to go to the men's room, I caught the maitre-d's eye. He came over.

"Is there a problem?"

"Mr. Clemenceau would like you to call his wife and ask her to join us." I handed him the card. He smiled tightly and hurried over to the phone.

Anton returned. Neither of us ate much of our meal. He glanced at his watch.

"I have ordered dessert and champagne on the yacht. Shall we go?"

"Not just yet."

I opened my purse and placed the black velvet case on the table.

"Anton, in a few minutes Giselle is going to walk in. And I'm going to tell her that you invited me to spend the night on your good friend's yacht."

His face went white. "What is the meaning of this?"

"The meaning is that you have only a few moments to, shall we say, pull your ass out of the sling it's in."

"This is outrageous." He took out a handkerchief and patted his face.

"Just hand me the envelope and take the diamond and

we'll call it even."

He stiffened. "I will deny everything."

I took his hand in mine. "I suppose you will. I'm wondering what other explanation there could be for a married man having a private dinner with a young woman after he lied to his wife about what he was doing this evening?"

I had no way of knowing if he lied but figured odds were in my favor he had.

"She will not believe you."

"Anton, how could I possibly know you have a friend named Phillipe who owns a yacht?"

"This is extortion. I will report this to the police." He was quite indignant.

I sipped some water, steeling myself. "Really? And tell them what, exactly?"

He blinked several times, then reached into his pocket and handed me the envelope. I slid the black leather case toward him.

"Thank you." I gathered my things. "It was a pleasure doing business with you. By the way, why don't you give the necklace to Giselle?"

Anton wouldn't call the police. There would be too many questions and no good answers.

I was a block away before my heart stopped thumping. I took a deep breath, removed the check from my purse and took one long look at it. There was no doubting the irony that Luther's gift provided the funds to restore *Dreamboat*.

I smiled, stuffed the check back into my purse and headed home.

44

Fifteen hundred dollars went a long way.

Within two weeks, Otis rebuilt the engine, found a used refrigerator, stove, generator, marine radio and GPS. We had three hundred dollars left and I kept it for trip provisions.

A. had good days and bad days. At first, more good than bad, but as August drew to a close more bad than good.

Except for working on the boat, I spent all my time with him. I prepared breakfast and dinner. I borrowed some cookbooks from the main house so his meals would consist of more than soft-boiled eggs, perfectly made or not.

"We have to talk about the trip," I said while clearing the dinner table one night.

"Lila, you understand that some might call this idea of yours the height of madness."

"It is! We'll sail along the coast and dock at Key West for the night. Bright and early the next morning we'll set out for the

Tortugas. "

He laughed softly. "Simple as that?"

"Hundreds of people sail there. I've got tons of info from the Internet."

"And what happens if the engine blows?"

"The engine is fine now."

"Or we hit a storm."

"We'll check the weather before we depart."

He stared at me for a long moment. "You're not the least bit apprehensive, are you?"

"No." I was terribly apprehensive but not admitting it seemed the best course of action.

"Why are you so determined to do this?" he asked.

"Because it's important to you. And because years from now I don't want to be talking about how I could have sailed to the Dry Tortugas but didn't do it because it seemed like a strange or odd or foolish thing to do." I took a deep breath. "I guess I've decided I'm too young to start collecting regrets."

And so, without A. ever saying that we were going to do it, we made plans. Every day we'd talk about the charts and make lists of things to remember and things to do. He used his wooden boats to point out the parts of the ship, the proper names and how they worked.

I don't think he really decided to make the trip until he saw *Dreamboat*. I insisted that he would see the boat when it was shipshape. And not before.

Otis picked us up and drove us to the dock. The boat bobbed gently on the water. The hull was dark green with a red waterline. The cabin was cream colored and the brightwork just sparkled.

A. stood there for the longest time without saying a word, then placed his hand on my shoulder and gave it a squeeze.

"I'll be damned," he murmured.

I walked him around to the stern. "We named it *Dreamboat*."

"Might I ask why?"

"It's what the women at the Club Coral call you."

He laughed softly and shook his head.

We climbed aboard and I gave him the grand tour. He asked tons of questions, a lot of technical stuff Otis had to answer. Finally, he stood at the bow and stared out at the calm, endless ocean. I glanced at Otis, who indicated I was to just bide my time.

After what seemed an eternity, he turned to me and said, "If you're bound and determined then."

After that, A. was very hard on me, questioning me

repeatedly about all sorts of matters relating to the operation of the boat. I learned words like *jib* and *forestay* and *boom vang*. All of which seemed fairly straightforward.

The this-and-that about the sails and wind was another matter entirely.

He took a model boat and set it on the table. He cut little paper arrows to represent the wind direction and would move them around and make me call out the proper response.

"Bear away," I'd say.

"Head down."

"Right. Head down. I've got it, honest."

One night, after dinner, we were sitting on the patio. The air was warm and the smell of oranges hung in the air. He had sliced up some provolone and apples. He wore tan silk pants with suspenders and brown leather loafers and his singlet T-shirt.

"I was thinking we should depart September fifteenth, weather permitting, which means we reach the Tortugas on or about the eighteenth."

"The eighteenth?"

He cocked his head and eyed me. "I don't think this trip should be just about me," he began. "I think it should also be about sailing to the Dry Tortugas on your eighteenth birthday."

It had been a long time since an adult had given more than a second thought about what might be meaningful to me.

"Yes," I replied, "that would be great."

He sipped some wine. "One important detail I had almost forgotten. You told me you have a passport."

"Yes."

"You need to bring it along."

"Why?"

"Because if one sails upon the ocean it is prudent to carry a passport. International waters and all," he explained. He said it in a casual 'oh and by the way' manner and I didn't think to question him further. He glanced at his watch. "I'm going to call it a night."

After he went inside, I stayed around and nibbled on the cheese. The entire matter of my eighteenth birthday had faded in my memory over the last month but his comment reminded me that on the eighteenth I would no longer be a minor. It meant I could buy cigarettes and vote, of course, but most importantly, it meant Mother no longer had any legal control over me. In some respects, that was cool, you know, but bottom-line, it also meant that I needed to fend for myself.

To be honest, the prospect was terrifying to me but I was happy that A. would be around to help me with the fending.

45

It was heartbreaking to watch A. deteriorate before my eyes. His headaches grew stronger and he popped Excedrin like candy. He slept a lot and it became much harder for him to focus.

The morning of our shakedown cruise I arrived to find three large piles of his belongings set out in the cottage.

One pile I'll call the metal pile, because it contained three old brass navigation instruments, two silver Leica cameras, four pocket watches and a windproof brass cigarette lighter.

The second pile was the leather pile, with two wallets, a portfolio and a worn leather shoulder bag. The final pile was the writing pile, with the collected works of Shakespeare, and Bullfinches mythology, along with four tortoise-shell fountain pens.

A. was pulling a shot of espresso.

"What's all this?" I asked.

"Just a little housekeeping," he said.

The big travel trunk sat with the lid already open.

"Be a dear and pack that detritus in the trunk," he said, sitting down.

"Are you taking this trunk on the trip?" I asked as I placed the piles inside.

"No," he answered. "Just close the lid and pull it over

near the door."

I did as he asked.

Finally, we took the boat out for a shakedown cruise. Otis came along but he just drank beer and sunned himself.

It was a magnificent day. The breeze pushed smiling wavelets across the surface of the ocean.

I trimmed the sails and spun the winch as A. barked orders. The boat cut through the ocean like a knife through butter. I did not find my sea legs until we passed the channel markers.

We made a wide circle and at one point, the land disappeared from view. Otis took the wheel and A. motioned me into the cabin.

We spent forty-five minutes talking about the chart. When you're out on the ocean with nothing but the horizon, navigation is a bit more complicated. However, I kept my wits about me and answered questions to his satisfaction.

I took the helm and he stood next to me, pointing at the compass and explaining the nuances of piloting.

I loved sailing. It's as close as anyone can get to feeling completely free. I could definitely imagine myself as a sea-faring gal.

There were sounds I will never forget. The first was the

constant creaking of the boat, like someone sneaking up wooden stairs. The second was the gurgle of the water against the hull. and lastly, the sound the sails snapping in the wind.

After two hours, we headed back. The engine spit diesel fumes as we motored toward the dock. I hopped off and tied the boat to the mooring.

"I guess it's best to gather provisions," A. said.

"Aye, aye sir," I said, snapping off a salute.

Against all odds, A. and I were about to sail to the Dry Tortugas.

46

This isn't really a how-to-do-it book on sailing, so suffice it to say we set off at dawn on the appointed day. A. and Otis had a long talk on the dock but it was clear they didn't want to me hear what they were talking about. Otis gave A. a big hug and we were off.

I noticed that Otis had lashed a seven-foot dinghy to the gunwales on the stern. Obviously, a lifeboat in case something went wrong.

There was a moment when A. went down below, the wind suddenly shifted, and we headed upwind. I had to act quickly or we would be in the no-go zone, meaning we would be trying to sail directly into the wind, an impossible feat.

"Antonio!" I called out.

He didn't answer but for some reason I didn't panic. I tacked just as he taught me. I trimmed the sails and close-hauled until the wind was behind me. And the *Dreamboat* ran, fast and quick.

At that moment, I learned a life's lesson. It is better to adjust to the changes around you than be bullheaded enough to sail right into whatever obstacle you faced. You needed to be aware of those changes and act quickly and with purpose and instead of the wind going out of your sails, you could race away from whatever threatened you.

Just then, Antonio emerged onto the deck.

"I did it! It worked just like you said it would!"

He flashed a big smile. I felt so damn good. This man had come into my life out of nowhere, rescued me from that steamy underworld and the man with the dog collar, and put me at the helm of a sailboat racing through the ocean. I had no way of repaying him, of course, other than devoting my life to finding him the best damn brain tumor guy in the world.

We made Key West without further incident. My face was raw from the wind but I was otherwise in good shape. A. was another matter, however. He spent a lot of time down below and I assumed he was flat on his back. But he came up just as Key

West came into view.

We switched to engine power and he took the wheel. There were massive cruise ships anchored everywhere. We made our way to the City Marina, passing under the Fleming Key Bridge. We berthed at Slip 32 next to a floating concrete dock. We tied off and Antonio handled the rental fee.

I showered while he replenished our water supply. I put on a pair of white shorts and a red blouse. I went up on deck and waited until he appeared in his chinos, a flowered shirt and a straw Panama hat.

We strolled through the streets of Key West. We stopped at Hemingway's House and Museum. I petted some cats in the gardens. Then we walked over to the Butterfly Conservancy and walked through a tropical jungle with parrots squawking and all manner of butterflies fluttering about. We sat for a while in Mallory Square and listened to the street musicians play.

Finally, we walked down Duval Street and stopped at Sloppy Joe's.

"This was Hemingway's favorite bar," A. said as he ordered himself a scotch. I settled for lemonade.

"Did you know that the cats at the Hemingway House all have six toes? They're called —." I fumbled for the word.

"Polydactyl."

"Now why does it not surprise me you would know that?"

"Lucky guess."

"Right." I sipped some lemonade. "How do you feel?" I asked.

He snickered. "As fine as a dying man can be."

"It's nothing to joke about."

He stared into his scotch for while, and then said softly, "I've made one or two fortunes and lost them along the way. Way I figure it, I've done the things I wanted to do and seen the places I wanted to see and I'll own up to every stupid decision I made. I don't have any regrets."

"Good. Neither do I." I lifted my glass. "To a life of no regrets." He lifted his glass and tapped it against mine.

We ate fried calamari, conch fritters and famous Sloppy Joe's sloppy joes and Cajun fries. I stuffed food into my mouth and went on about the wind and the ocean and how wonderful it all was. He listened, patiently, as he always did when my enthusiasm bubbled up like warm Coke from a two-liter bottle.

Finally, I patted my belly. "I ate like a pig."

"You must have a slice of key lime pie with raspberry sauce."

"I'm stuffed," I protested.

"I insist," he said and ordered me a slice.

"What did you do in Istanbul?" I asked as I dug into the pie. "Were you like a spy?"

He glanced off into the distance. "Let's just say I was available to do certain things that needed to be done."

I pointed the fork at him. "You were a spy."

He laughed.

Being as I was under twenty-one, bar policy required that I depart before nine-thirty. I was tired anyway. Antonio paid the bill. It had been a wonderful day.

When we reached the entrance, he slipped his wallet into his back pocket and with the same motion grabbed my arm with his free hand and slumped to his knees, pulling me with him.

One of the hostesses saw what happened but before she could ask what was wrong I shouted, "Ambulance. Quick!"

47

I sat outside the emergency room for two hours.

Nurses and doctors came and went through the swinging double doors. Those doors reminded of that night at Club Coral and brought a brief smile to my face.

I sat in the single row of chairs that lined the wall. At the end of the row, a gray-haired woman sat with a handkerchief clutched in her hand. She dabbed her eyes now and then.

Finally, a doctor appeared. He approached the older woman and asked her something. She shook her head. He saw me and walked over.

He was maybe thirty-five. His breath smelled like spearmint. He had a clipboard and clicked a ball-point pen continuously.

"Are you with Mr. Garibaldi?"

"Yes."

"I'm Doctor Weidner." He extended his hand. I shook it.

"I'm Lila."

"Are you related to him?"

"He's my uncle. How is he?"

"Conscious. His vital signs are stable. We'll move him to regular room for overnight observation. Does he have any immediate family we can contact? A wife? Brother?"

"He just has me."

Dr. Weidner looked at his clipboard. I figured he had the information I had given to the bored woman behind the computer when he was admitted.

"My parents live in West Palm," he said and then added, "South Ocean Boulevard. Nice address." He looked back at the clipboard. "Normally, I would recommend a battery of tests for your uncle but it doesn't appear that he has health insurance, so that might—"

"Uncle Antonio and I are sailing to the Dry Tortugas for my eighteenth birthday," I said quickly. "He's scheduled for a battery of tests when we get back."

A sort of half-smile formed on Dr. Widener's lips. "I always wanted to sail."

His beeper sounded. He checked it quickly. "Hey, good luck. And happy birthday."

He hurried off down the hallway.

I found my way to A's room. It was a double but there was no one in the second bed.

"Hi," I said, taking his hand. "Had me worried there."

I gave his hand a squeeze. In the dim light of the room he looked fragile.

"Doctor says you're stable. Good to go." I took a deep breath. "When we get back, I am going to find you the very best octopus brain tumor specialist in the country. And I want you to promise you'll see him."

He looked at me for a very long time and then said, "If that will make you happy."

It did make me happy because I knew that somewhere in the world was a brilliant genius who was going to stop the octopus brain tumor from taking A. away from me.

I was going to find that doctor.

"Come by in the morning. We've things to do," he said.

"I'm not going anywhere."

I pulled up a chair and held his hand until he fell asleep. I slept fitfully, waking with a start every few minutes.

A nurse came by to check on him every once in a while. The first time she whispered, "You are not supposed to be here. Visiting hours are over," but didn't push the matter.

In my few waking moments I wondered what I would do if he fainted on the last leg of our journey, out in the ocean, far away from help. I figured I'd radio the Coast Guard and they'd show up in plenty of time.

Looking back, I can see I just didn't want to think about his brain tumor or any complications that would arise. Sort of an out-of-mind, out-of-sight scenario.

We were going to get to the Dry Tortugas and then we were going home.

And everything would be right-as-rain.

48

He was discharged in the morning. A. didn't have hospitalization, and we didn't have cash or a credit card to cover the bill. The discharge lady seemed perturbed by this but produced some paperwork. I was tired and the clerk talked very fast but the paperwork had something to do with a federal law and Medicare and being indigent. A. just signed it.

As we stepped out into the morning sun he said, "There's someone I need to see."

We went down to the docks and stopped at a place called Gulf Coast Boat Brokers. Inside, a barrel-chested man with a grey, unkempt beard puffed on a black cigar as he leafed through the morning paper. When he saw A., he nearly fell off his chair.

"Holy shit and shinola! I can't fucking believe it! Garibaldi, you dog!" He came over and gave A. a big hug, slapping him on the back. "The last time I saw you was—when the fuck was it anyway?"

He smiled and a gold front tooth flashed.

"Jocko, let me introduce you to Lila Thibideaux, of the Louisiana Thibideaux," A. said.

He gave me the once over and then glanced at A.

"Lila is my business partner."

"Strictly business," I added.

We walked over to Slip 32.

Jocko removed the cigar from his mouth and whistled softly. "Now that's not something you see every day. Thirty-five if it's an inch."

"Sailed her down from Palm Beach," I added. "Engine rebuilt, hull and deck stripped to bare wood and refinished. Sails are in perfect working order. New generator, too. And it's a Randolph. Commissioned 1929."

A laugh fairly burst from Jocko's chest.

"You got a real little tar here," Jocko said. He climbed on board and disappeared into the cabin. Twenty minutes later, he emerged and rejoined us.

"It's a Randolph, for certain." He scratched at his beard. "Where'd you pick her up?"

"It's salvage."

"Brought it back from the dead, did you?"

"Lila did."

"And I've got the calluses to prove it," I added.

"What do you think she's worth?" A. asked.

Jocko removed his cigar and blew out a long breath. "Shit, at auction? Who knows? Thirty-grand if the right collector showed up. Twenty on a bad day. Hard to say anymore."

"How about wholesale?"

Jocko rubbed the back of his sunburned neck. "Economy's gone to hell. On a cash deal, I suppose eight, eight-five. Most folks are nervous about a boat this old. Big spenders want fiberglass."

Jocko picked bits of tobacco from his tongue then spit into the ocean. "Are you thinking of selling it?"

"No," I replied quickly.

"Just wondering," A. replied. They shook hands and A. put his arm around Jocko's shoulders and led him away. They talked in hushed tones for a few moments and shook hands.

"You're not going to sell it, are you?" I asked. Frankly, I was a little peeved about A.'s sidebar with Jocko.

"No."

Before we set out, we stopped at a grocery store. A. bought a bottle of wine, fresh sea bass, a loaf of French bread, fresh fruit and vegetables.

Our larder was full enough, but he seemed bound and determined to gather a number of very specific things. He did this without any list, which just proved to me that his octopus tumor hadn't really hurt his brain at all.

49

The winds were fair and uncomplicated and we made excellent time. It was a perfect day. Not a cloud in the sky. The green-blue ocean just stretched on forever.

We were a perfect team. I provided the boundless enthusiasm and A. the calm, measured judgment. We experienced the wind and sun together but really didn't say much.

Around four o'clock we dropped anchor at the southern tip of the Marquesas Keys.

I took a swim. Being in the ocean gives you a real sense of the insignificance of man in the face of nature. The ocean swells beneath you and you just bob along, helpless to do anything about it.

We turned in early and were up the next day again at dawn. A. seemed absolutely fine.

"This is it," I said as I hoisted the anchor. "Today we hit the Dry Tortugas."

It took nearly all day to get there. The winds were unpredictable and we ran into several short but hard rainstorms.

It was not until dusk that A. motioned to the island coming into view on the port side.

"We're here?"

"We have arrived."

I don't know how to describe the feeling that came over me. All the calluses and sore muscles and planning and cajoling had led me to this point and place in time.

"We did it! We sailed to the Dry Tortugas!"

I threw my arms around him, gave him a big hug, and inhaled his scent of bay rum and for a long moment, I didn't ever want to let go. But I did.

In the distance sat a massive fort illuminated by spotlights. I imagined Buford Thibideaux trying to run his guns past the booming canons.

We went about a mile past the fort and dropped anchor.

A. turned to me. "Lila, I believe that there are certain moments in life which call for a touch of elegance. This is one of those moments. I shall wear my tuxedo and you shall wear that black dress you are so fond of. We shall celebrate our success and your birthday in one fell swoop."

"It's the seventeenth."

"What's a day among friends?"

It ended up being a perfect night.

By the time I showered, did my hair, put on makeup, A. had cooked up the sea bass and made a fresh salad and a fruit parfait. He wore his tuxedo and looked quite handsome and healthy.

A. opened a bottle of wine and poured me some in a plastic cup.

"May all good things come your way."

"Back to you," I replied. I finished my cup and refilled it. "Glad we came?"

"I shall write a grand entry in my diary about this day."

We laughed. The amazing thing was that if you talked to him and watched him, he didn't seem sick at all.

I sipped more wine. "Tomorrow we go ashore. Up to the fort. Maybe buy a souvenir. A T-shirt, decal, or something, you know, act like *touristas*. Then we set sail for home."

I was light-headed from the wine and a bit wobbly. I wandered over to the gunwale.

"You know, I couldn't have imagined a better birthday than this, even though it's not technically my birthday."

When I turned, A. was bent over, hands on his knees. I ran to him.

"Is it bad?"

He held up his hand. "Just a passing twinge."

After a few moments, he stood and walked to the bow. I joined him.

"Why did Aunt Rowena let you live in the cottage?"

He massaged his forehead. "It likely surprises you to know she and I were once, as they say, an 'item'."

"Get out! I can't imagine you and Aunt Rowena, you know—."

"Ah," he said, growing expansive, "she was a spitfire. You remind me of her, to tell the truth."

"Don't say that."

He held up a finger. "She was twenty-six at the time and I a bit older. She was headstrong, bound and determined to have her way. She seduced me with her Southern belle accent and oh-so-proper ways."

I had a hard time imagining Aunt Rowena being twenty-six. I shuddered to think I'd end up same as her.

"One more question. Why did you agree to look after me?"

"To save you from the man in the dog collar, dear," he replied with all seriousness. We looked at each other and tried to keep from laughing but finally we had one of those long, silly laughing spells. When it ended, I had to wipe the tears from my eyes.

Darkness had fallen but the full moon cast a shimmering avenue across the water to our boat.

There was only one thing I needed to make my birthday complete.

"Mr. Garibaldi, may I have this dance?" I curtsied.

"Only if you favor me with a song."

He turned and bowed, then took my hand. I sang the *Tennessee Waltz*. I stumbled a bit, being as I was essentially drunk on my feet but A. had a way of spreading his grace over you like fairy dust.

"Are we waltzing?"

"Indeed we are."

"So tell me, how much did those women pay you to dance?"

"Ten dollars."

"They got off cheap."

He twirled me elegantly and our waltz ended.

"I've had too much to drink," I said, feeling a bit dizzy.

He walked away and stood with his back to me. In the distance, spotlights bathed the walls of the old fort.

I joined him.

"Thanks. For everything," I said.

"It was my distinct pleasure, Lila Valentine Thibideaux."

I looked over at him. I don't know if it was the light or what, but I could swear his eyes were moist.

The moon was full. The waves lapped softly against the boat. The warm breeze caressed us. The moment seemed both very real and completely unreal at the same time. I suppose all of us have that moment in time when everything just seems to make sense.

Not another word was said.

I left him on deck, staring into the darkness.

As I flopped down on the bed, I was certain that

everything was going to work out and we would sail together for many years to come, free from what haunted us.

50

I woke just after dawn and stumbled into the head. I took a long pee and then swallowed some aspirin to relieve my hangover.

"Antonio?" I called as I climbed onto the deck.

I remember every detail of that morning. A gauzy curtain of mist shrouded the boat. When I glanced out to where the fort used to be, there was nothing to be seen. At first, I thought it was simply because of the mist. However, when I checked the GPS, I realized our position had changed sometime during the night.

I checked the anchor and it was still seated, so Antonio had moved the boat while I slept.

Out of the corner of my eye, I saw the dinghy was missing. I shouted out his name several times as I walked the gunwales, figuring he'd maybe gone for a swim, though now that seems like a stupid idea.

Then I saw the rope tied to the rear ladder. At the end of the rope, bobbing in the water, was the dinghy. A was in the dinghy, still dressed in his tuxedo, arms crossed over his chest, just lying there.

I laughed at first, sort of a snickering half-guffaw.

"What are you doing?" I yelled as climbed down the ladder and pulled the dinghy close.

I climbed onto the boat and shook him gently. "Antonio, come on. Rise and shine. It's *tourista* day."

He didn't respond.

Then it hit me. Like a ton of bricks. My mouth went dry. My heart pounded. I leaned over and put a finger under his nose. He wasn't breathing. I tried to find his pulse to no avail. His skin was cold. All the color had drained from his face.

I fell backwards, right on my rear end. I sat there, my legs looped over the seat.

I wailed out a single word. "No!"

For the longest time, I sat in that awkward position and wept, the tears pouring down. I finally clambered back over the seat. I wiped the tears from my face, and then I laid my cheek against his chest and admitted the awful truth.

A.: Galahad to my Guinevere, Achilles to my Helen, Higgins to my Eliza, was gone forever.

As I said, his arms were crossed against his chest. In his right hand was an envelope. His left fist was tightly clenched.

I peeled his fingers back to reveal a small glass vial. I held it to my nose and recoiled at the bitter smell.

I removed the envelope from his hand. I took the glass

vial too. I climbed out of the dinghy and back on board. I sat down on the deck and pulled my legs up against my chest. For about a minute, I shivered and sniffled. I was in the middle of the worst nightmare imaginable.

I opened the envelope and removed the letter. He typed it before we left.

My dearest Lila,

Belladona. Supposedly used to poison the troops of Marcus Antonious during the Parthian Wars. When Duncan was king of Scotland, the soldiers of Macbeth poisoned an entire army of invading Danes. (We did not get to Shakespeare. I hope you will read, at the very least, "Romeo and Juliet.")

I came to Sea Spray to die in that small cottage. Rowena had no idea of my condition. She never asked. Such is the nature of long friendships.

My notion of sailing here was an old man's final grasp at his youth. A fool's errand at best. Your indefatigable energy and boundless optimism convinced me that a fool's errand was a perfectly acceptable pursuit for an old fool.

I have spent my life doing exactly as I pleased and so it should not surprise you that I have chosen the time, place and method of my demise.

But the plot has not yet played out, my dear. One good turn deserves another, as they say, and so please find the leather document holder beneath my mattress. If you wish to return my favors, follow the directions to the letter.

Antonio

51

I went into the cabin and sure enough, beneath his mattress was an old leather document folder. Inside was a single sheet of paper.

```
1.   Leave my body in dinghy. Douse with the liquid
from the gas can marked with an 'X'.
2.   Fire flare gun, found in emergency pack on wall.
3.   Untie dinghy.
4.   Motor back to Key West. Coordinates are on
chart.
5.   Moor boat at Slip 32.
```

I stared at the letter, completely numb.

There I was, barefoot in my wrinkled little black dress, hair looking like a bird's nest, face puffy and splotched. The man who had saved me from a life of ruin was dead by his own hand, floating in a dinghy in the middle of the ocean.

He had left me instructions on how to burn his body, an act I was certain was illegal.

Obviously, I could drag his body back on board and take it back to Key West. And then what? Put his body in the county morgue until I found a funeral home to take care of him without being paid? Maybe Aunt Rowena would have covered the cost but she was in Bar Harbor and Harold was in England. Trust me, if Antonio had dropped over from a heart attack and left no final instructions, I would have done whatever needed to be done to get him a proper burial. However, that was not the current scenario in which I found myself.

In my mind, it boiled down to one simple fact. This man

had been there in my hour of greatest need. He had protected me and made my life richer in countless ways. He had saved me from a journey down the road to ruin, even though he wasn't blood and had no obligation to act as he did. Maybe he pitied me but ultimately what he did was an act of human kindness.

The only thing he ever asked in return for that kindness was that I burn his dead body in the middle of the ocean. I don't know what anyone else would have done, but to me there was only one answer I could have to his request.

I figured with his mysterious past he had some special formula in that can. Once I fired the flare gun into the dinghy there was a white-hot burn so intense I had to turn away.

I untied the dinghy and headed back to Key West. For a brief instant, a True Crime television scenario, starring me, flashed through my mind. I sort of half-smiled, you know, from the irony of it all.

But I could not help myself and after a mile or so, I had to look back. The sun had not yet risen and the air was still gray but I saw steady white flame and the dark outline of the dinghy. Then, almost without warning, the dingy slipped beneath the waves. The white flame seemed to linger on the surface for a brief moment, like A.'s spirit or soul or aura or whatever you want to call that special life force I do believe we all possess.

Then the flame disappeared.

Bottom line, the way I figure it, was that Antonio was a hopeless romantic.

And if you are going to be romantic, hopeless is absolutely the way to go.

Hands down.

52

It was nearly three by the time I arrived in Key West. When I pulled into Slip 32, I was stunned to see Otis leaning against a dock post, arms crossed, puffing calmly on his pipe.

I waved and tossed the line to him. He tied off the boat and I jumped down onto the dock. I threw my arms around him and held on for the longest time.

"Now, now," he said softly.

"You knew, didn't you?" I said as I stepped back.

"Like I said, me and Mr. G. go back a long way."

"Why didn't he let me find someone who could get rid of that tumor?"

"There was no hope. Oh, he could keep on living, but it was only a matter of time before he became blind or crippled. And he just wasn't about to let that happen."

I leaned against the hull and stared out at the ocean. "What am I going to do now?"

It really did feel like an entire episode of my life had ended and the next page was blank.

Otis pulled an envelope out from his back pocket and tapped it against his palm.

He smiled that big Otis smile. "You think Mr. G. would leave you high and dry?"

He handed the envelope to me.

"Inside you will find enough cash to stake you and a plane ticket to Florence."

"Why am I going to South Carolina?"

Otis chuckled. "Florence, Italy, my dear."

"Italy!"

"There's a phone number inside. When you land, call it. Mrs. Monteverdi will pick you up."

My mind was truly spinning.

"Otis, I don't understand any of this."

He glanced at his watch. "You're got about four hours until the plane leaves. When I sell the boat, you'll get your share, like I promised. Come on now, get a move on."

I climbed back onto the boat. I pulled off my dress and showered. Then I stuffed the black dress into the backpack and pulled on a pair of jeans, a white T and tennis shoes. My hair was wet and that couldn't be helped at that particular moment.

As I grabbed my backpack, I noticed A.'s Panama hat hanging on a wooden peg.

I tried it on and I must say it I looked good in it. The fact that it was a smidgen too large just added to its flair. When I checked inside the zipper pocket of my bag to make sure my passport was there, I found the sunglasses Marla had given me.

I put them on, symbolically taking the two people who had saved me from the mess that was my life to the adventure of my new life, which apparently waited for me in Italy.

Outside again, I joined Otis. He was at the end of the dock, where a taxi idled. I gave him a hug and a kiss on the cheek.

"Otis, before you sell that boat, take a picture and send it to me."

I got into the cab. Otis leaned into the window.

"You take care of yourself, Lila Valentine Thibideaux."

"I will." The taxi pulled away.

I didn't look back.

53

I slept most of the way on the flight to Florence.

When I woke, I imagined Aunt Rowena standing in front of a six-foot portrait of me and saying, "This is Lila Thibideaux, my bastard niece. She lived abroad for many years. She was accused of acts too disgusting to mention in proper society, but was, of course, fully exonerated." I laughed aloud at the thought.

Aunt Rowena may have taken me in for all the wrong reasons, but the fact was she had. Even though she left the day I arrived, if she had stayed, none of what happened would have happened. Sometimes things just work out for the best.

I took good care of the two letters A. left me. I told myself I did what I thought was right considering the circumstances and would have to live with the consequences. Of course, given my life experience to that point, I knew there would be. Consequences, that is.

I did what Otis instructed when we landed. Mrs. Monteverdi was in her sixties, a striking woman with shining black hair and a ready smile. After she kissed me on both cheeks, she pinched them.

The trunk that A. had me pack and set by the door? It was delivered some time later. Seems Otis had sent it along per A.'s instructions.

You know the rest of the story. It is nearly dawn now as I finish these last words.

Try as I might, I cannot think of a profound lesson to be drawn from this story. In the end, I decided to let it speak for itself.

There are those who will think most of it is the result of my overactive imagination and may not believe a word of it.

I could care less because I know it is true.

Come to think of it, this story isn't about me anyway.

Not at all.

The End

www.ingramcontent.com/pod-product-compliance
Lightning Source LLC
Chambersburg PA
CBHW070605130626
46556CB00001B/280